GHETTO GIRLS IV

Young Luv

ESSENCE BESTSELLING AUTHOR
ANTHONY WHYTE

ISBN: 978-0-9792816-6-2

Novel by Anthony Whyte
Edited by Clarence Haynes
Creative Direction & Design by Jason Claiborne
Photography by GlamBang.com

Augustus Publishing paperback July 2009
www.augustuspublishing.com

ACKNOWLEDGMENTS

First of all I'd like to thank my connect: (The Augustus Publishing Manuscript Team). Jason Claiborne, Tamiko Maldonado, Joy Leftow. Good looking out, Clarence Haynes, Bobby Nickels, Sumya Ojakli, David Wilk, Bill Gladstone,Yolanda Palmer, Antonia, Kyle Harris. Elaine Hyatt, thank you for the advice. I also want to thank the book vendors on the street corners, Divine, Nel, Najee. I'd like to say, thanks to the booksellers, wholesalers and distributors in stores: Books In The Hood and Hue man. Jay-Clay we've come a long way, still doing it big, the Augustus Media Group. Most of all, I want to say; thanks, to you the customers and the many readers I write for. Much love for looking-out and pitching in your support for me and all my peers. From the start this is Black Art, Hip Hop fiction. Read on.

One Love, Anthony Whyte

ARCTIC GLACIER

PROLOGUE

"In order for me to be immortal all weak-ass muthafuckas and bitches must die..."

The bodyguard in the rear reached for his weapon and was felled by the sudden blast of two guns.

"If you ain't heard, I said, weak muthafuckas and bitch-ass-niggas must die...!" the angered voice chanted.

More gunshots exploded, hitting the bodyguard up front. He lay crumpled as a pool of blood formed around his head. The girls darted for cover and heard the gruff voice shouting at them. Eric stood looking baffled by the commotion.

"No, no I ain't gon' kill y'all yet. Gi-Gi-Git da fuck back here, ya-ya-yall b-b-bitches! Yeah, nigga. I-I-I wa-want ya to kno-

kno' wh-wh-who da fu-fu-fuck I is. Then I'm a pu-pu-pump lead in ya bitch-ass! It's me, Li-Li-Lil' Long, muthafuckas! Remember me? I'm the one y'all bust 'em caps in the last time. Yeah, that's right. Luck was on my side."

Coco, Deedee, Josephine and Eric, along with his two bodyguards, had just exited Club IV. The atmosphere had been electric inside. Exhausted from the night's activity, the group was on their way to the parking lot. They froze when they heard the menacing chant.

"That's right. In order for me to survive y'all weak ass muthafuckas must die! Die! Die!"

The shaken group held their breaths. Loud music was pumping and club kids were heard shouting in the club. Coco and Josephine had energized them with a high-octane midnight concert rapping and singing. Silky Black and the Chop Shop Crew got busy rapping and took the excitement generated by the girls to another level. The club-heads wanted more and were still going wild even after the performers left the stage. Cameras lights went off in rapid succession as the girls clowned and posed while leaving the club.

"I'm mad hungry, yo," Coco said, joining Deedee, who was walking away with Eric and the bodyguards.

"That makes two of us," Deedee said as she smiled and hugged Coco.

Coco stopped, pulled out a cigarette and lit up. They watched Josephine glamming it up for the paparazzi.

"She's killing it, yo," Coco said, pulling on her cigarette.

"Yes, she's really feeling herself, huh?" Deedee said. Coco couldn't help but notice the contempt dripping off Deedee's lips.

"Do I detect a little hater-ation, yo?" Coco laughed and Deedee joined in.

"I'm just tired."

"Me too, yo," Coco admitted, pulling on the cigarette.

Later, Josephine, trailed by a couple of flashbulbs, hurried outside to join the others. Out in the early morning air, they could hear Rakim spitting in the background.

It's been a long time /I shouldn't have left you…

Without a strong rhyme to step to…

Think on how many weak shows you slept through

Time's up… I'm sorry I kept you…

The lyrics were punctuated by gunshots and followed by surreal taunts from nemesis number one, Lil' Long.

"Yeah bitch-ass, where you gon' run now?"

"I-I-I wasn't involved, mister. I wasn't even in the city. I-I-I wasn't…" Josephine said, shuddering excitedly.

"Bitch, d-d-don'tcha kno' better'an to mock me? You better fall back over thurr with the rest of them 'fore I start witcha ya ass! Yeah muthafuckas, finally we meet ag'in," Lil' Long said, prancing around with two guns held high gloating. He aimed one point blank at Eric's dome and moved in closer.

"Let the girls go and—"

"And what, bitch ass nigga? Whatcha thunk? You gon' pay me off too? I know your ass been payin' for protection," Lil' Long said, getting front and center in Eric's face.

The girls tried to sneak away but Lil' Long whirled with a vicious glance directed at them.

"Don't even think about runnin' to the Range, bitches," he yelled. Lil' Long shot a glance back at Eric and said, "I've got bad news for ya. Da driver done stank-up da whole muthafuckin' place in thurr."

Lil' Long's laughter echoed eerily in the chill of the early morning air. Eric watched his assailant's every step. He wanted to get the girls out of harm's way.

"This beef's between me and you, man… it has nothing to do with anyone else," Eric said.

Lil' Long laughed as Eric spoke. He waved one of his guns side to side while keeping the other trained on the girls.

"Uh huh, it's got urrh-thing to do with these bitches and everyone your bitch-ass nigga knows. From your fiancée, right down to this fine ass black bitch me and my man ran-up-in was fam, dogs? I kno' ya ain't seen the way me and my man dug da bitch back out, so I'm a brake you off a lil' sho', you kno'? Encore, you unnerstan…? A lil' sump'n, sump'n, this is for makin' me wait so muthafuckin' long to kill y'all muthafuckin' asses already. But first I'm gonna do this…"

Two rounds punctuated Lil' Long's diatribe and Eric fell to the ground.

"Ugh… agh... shit! You shot me…" Eric shouted, grabbing his arm.

"Ouch, sorry my man. Think I miss? Just nick ya with a lil' flesh wound to warn ya fucking ass. Get used to the pain, nigga. I'm a make ya feel it. I ain' gon kill ya just yet, muthafucka. I'm a have some fun and I wanna make sure you stick around to enjoy the sho'. Ya smell me?"

He grabbed Deedee and pushed her to her knees. "Get on ya knees, bitch! Ya kno' what time it is. Grab up on this dick and start da brain show!"

Deedee hesitated. Fear registered on all their faces when Lil' Long shoved the gun in Deedee's terrified face. Lil' Long's figure loomed large over her as he pushed Deedee to her knees. Eric flinched but Lil' Long's guns were cocked and ready.

"Yeah muthafucka, jump! If ya don't wanna see this bitch brain me, then you can go six-feet in a box, bitch-ass. I waited a long time for this moment. Payback's a bitch!" Lil' Long turned his attention back to Deedee. "Reach up in thurr with them luscious lips and eat my dick, bitch! Then tell your uncle how good it taste, ya heard me bitch?" Lil' Long wore a smile, licking his lips. "What da fu-fuck! Get it nice and ha-hard bitch," Lil' Long said struggling with his stutter.

Revenge clouded his eyes and his breath came in gasps.

He was angry and impatiently pushed scared stiff Deedee's face into his crotch. She fumbled with her hands by her sides but silently refused to touch Lil' Long's hardening member.

"I'll pay you whatever you want man but please don't do this…" Eric pleaded.

"Shuddafuckup! Take it like a man and stop begging ya bitch-ass! Watch ya niece take real dick," Lil' Long said. He aimed the gun point blank at Eric's dome. "I was in jail dreaming about this moment, muthafucka. Yes I was…!"

"Why you wanna play us like that, yo?" Coco asked, staring at Lil' Long. "If you gonna kill us just get it over with. You ain't gotta torture us, yo."

Lil' Long pushed Deedee away and walked over closer to where Coco stood.

"Oh, bitch, I see it's true what they say about you, you do got a lot a heart, huh? You da shit, huh?"

"I'm saying yo…"

"Ya ain't allowed to speak. This my muthafuckin' world. I-I-I gi-gi-give the orders round here, bitch!" Lil' Long shouted and fired twice. Coco fell. Josephine tried to jump to her aid but Lil' Long grabbed her and shoved her to the asphalt.

"Bitch, you move and I'll kill ya fuckin' ass!" He aimed the guns at her dome.

Josephine's body seemed stuck in fear. His evil look left her frozen in tears. Deedee was still on her knees, crying and screaming loudly.

"He shot Coco..."

"Bitch, what ya doin' all that hollerin' for?" Lil' Long asked Deedee.

Josephine trembled with fear as she cried and watched. Both Eric and Coco were shot and bleeding. Eric was still conscious, but Coco was lying unconscious. Deedee resisted as Lil' Long held the back of her neck and furiously tried to shove his dick in her mouth through his Roca Wear. Lil' Long slapped her face so hard, Deedee fell backwards. He stood over with his guns ready.

"Ahight, I see ya gon sho' out cuz ya uncle, huh? Ahight, fu-fu-fuck it then bi-bi-bitch. You leave me no choice. I'm go-go-gonna give ya your d-d-death wish. In order for me to be immortal all y'all weak muthafuckas and bitches will have to—"

Suddenly there was an explosion.

"Oh shit... ugh..." Lil' Long grunted. .

He whirled and grabbed his shoulder. One of the guns fell from his grip. Eric immediately tried to reach for it.

"This is the police. Nobody move."

Lil' Long looked up. Recognizing the face, he smiled.

"Wha' ya shot me for, detective? I was doing y'all po-po a lil' fa-favor and ya-ya sh-shot me?"

"Oh yeah, what's your favor?" the detective asked, bending down and removing the gun from Lil' Long's clutch.

"I know y'all know that this da kingpin right thurr. Eric

Ascot. He's got the mob sewn up and he be ordering hits on muthafuckas left and right. Drugs, he running that..." Lil' Long paused to laugh. "Yeah, I'm a snitch on ya... fake-ass music producer." He continued laughing.

"Is it true, Ascot?" the detective asked.

"I don't know what he's talking about. He was trying to murder us. If I was connected, why did he... he just tried to rape my niece... again."

The detective's eyes followed Eric's stare to where Coco laid. Deedee joined Josephine and they were both crying over the fallen teen.

"Is it true? Did this piece o' shit try to rape you again?" the detective asked. Deedee nodded. The detective stared at the contortions of pain all over Eric's face.

"Who ya gon believe, my man? We partnas in this. He's the real kingpin behind all this!" Lil' Long shouted.

"Partners? No, we're not," the detective said with a sarcastic grin.

The detective watched the expression on Eric's face as he emptied the magazine in the body of Lil' Long.

"My partner was killed," the detective said. Lil' Long's body was in death's dance when the detective grabbed Eric's hand and tightened his fingers around the smoking gun. "I want you to know what it feels like to take a life and I want to know the reason my partner was murdered. Do we have a deal?" Kowalski asked.

Eric's answer was barely audible but the detective was satisfied. He was on his horn.

"Gunshots fired, two people hit. Officer needs assistance."

Kowalski gave the location and shoved the phone back in his pocket. Deedee walked over and hugged Eric. He was bleeding but still standing and holding on to the gun Kowalski had given him. Josephine sobbed softly with Coco's head quietly resting in her lap. The ambulance seemed to arrive with the quickness but it still felt like forever.

The medical technicians hurried Coco in and immediately started attending to her injury. The bullet had grazed Eric's arm and the injury didn't require hospitalization. The paramedics patched up his arm and the detective hauled him away to an unmarked car.

"Take the girls to the hospital," Eric said to the bodyguard. "I'll be in touch with you as soon as I can."

He sat in the backseat of the police car. Both Deedee and Josephine were teary eyed watching Eric being driven away.

"C'mon get in," the bodyguard said to the girls after hailing a cab. "Follow that ambulance."

Deedee and Josephine hopped in. The cab sped off in the early morning air, chasing the ambulance. There was hardly any traffic on the road and the taxi easily stayed behind the speeding ambulance. Once they reached the hospital, the girls jumped from the cab and raced to catch up with the EMT's who were already taking Coco through the emergency room door.

They kept walking behind the gurney, their heartbeat racing as Coco was carried beyond where they could enter. The security stepped in front of them.

"Are you family members?" His stare was friendly but firm.

"Yes…" Josephine said quickly.

"And you, young lady?" he asked, addressing Deedee, who was still staring straight ahead as if in a trance.

"No… I mean yes. No, she's our best friend…"

"You're gonna have to wait over in the waiting area until the doctors are through examining her," the security said pointing. "Wait over there. The nurse will call you soon enough."

"Thanks," Deedee responded as if by some remote force.

She was a wreck, her mind running a hundred miles an hour and her body exhausted trying to keep up. Deedee glanced at Josephine and wondered why the bullet hadn't hit her instead of Coco. Why Coco? She grimaced when Josephine's mouth started running. Deedee wanted to shut this mouthpiece down but was so tired she could only listen to the ranting.

"Why didn't you tell home-boy we were sisters? You know we down like that..." Josephine's voice trailed when she saw the look of concern clouding Deedee's face. "Coco's gonna fight through this," she continued. "I know her. You give her any type of chance and she's winning. That's just Coco."

Deedee glanced at Josephine and stared off. The incident replayed inside her head like a terrible nightmare. Her body quivered. While Josephine was confident about Coco's eventual recovery, Deedee was still finding it difficult to wrap her mind around the fact that Coco was even shot.

"Try calling her mother again," Deedee suggested.

CHAPTER 1

"I got that hard white lady…"

Ms. Harvey heard the recognizable pitch. She felt her heartbeat increasing and automatically her steps quickened, hurrying in the other direction. Ms. Harvey folded her arms around her slim, frail body. She gritted her teeth and tried to ignore the humming coming from deep inside the recesses of her mind. The same urge and familiar mental gnawing of wanting to fly far away had crept from her stomach, impeding her breathing. Sounds mixed with her fear came from her dry lips.

"I got it, oh boy…"

"I don't want none o' y'all sh—"

"This will make you feel real good, Ma."

Ms. Harvey walked on as the lure of getting high moved through her body. The thought of her last high left her feeling euphoric but uneasy. Ms. Harvey's legs went rubbery and her stroll slowed. She appeared to be suffering shortness of breath when she stopped and looked back.

"We can go around the corner…keep it on da low-low."

Ms. Harvey tried hard to stay on the straight and narrow since making a pact with her daughter in early spring. It was the beginning of what she hoped to be a nice summer. It was past midnight and she had decided to take a walk. Her daughter was in the club celebrating successfully graduating from high school with friends. Ms. Harvey was very proud of her daughter and earlier relished the accolades bestowed on Coco. It was late Friday night and Ms. Harvey couldn't stay inside her apartment. She was excited and wanted to share her daughter's story with peeps from the neighborhood.

Coco gave a wonderful and moving valedictorian speech. She lauded her mother, which lifted Ms. Harvey's swag to dizzying heights. So she went about the neighborhood on a crowing mission. Ms. Harvey soon found herself outside a local bar, a few blocks down from her apartment building. While spreading the news to anyone who would listen, someone bought her a drink and another.

In her walk back home, she thought of how Coco lived up to her end of the agreement they'd struck. She wanted to keep her end of the bargain but Ms. Harvey was alone and temptation inched closer. It was like a silver back gorilla, prowling and looming larger and larger in the form of cheap cocaine.

"Crack is no good for you," she said.

Rachel Harvey was alone in familiar haunts with old

friends and old habits. Drinking alcohol made her decisions even more erratic and she knew being out on the street after midnight, anything could happen. In the hopes of an extended drug-cipher, her friends copped jumbos of crack.

"You gonna get you a lil' sump'n, right Rachel?"

It was all up to her now.

"I got it right here, the best thing for you…"

Ms. Harvey had heard it before. The counselors had tried to prepare her for moments like this. Couple weeks in a residential and a few months in an outpatient program had saved her life. The last time she binged, her heart had literally stopped. She didn't want to binge.

"Nothing good happens after midnight," she whispered.

Ms. Harvey could hear the counselor's voice buzzing in her head. She remembered all the steps to maintain her sobriety. Trying to walk the walk, her strut slowed. She felt the yearning overtaking her senses and soon it was no use running. Too weak to fight, she stopped, looked at the pitcher and gave the proverbial nod.

A few minutes later, Ms. Harvey and a couple of her drug-related friends were coughing up a storm while sucking the crack-pipe. Sweat drained profusely from her pores as the rock went from yellow to bright red. She puffed, took a breath and inhaled deeply,.

"Ah yes, I'm ready to get it on…" she hissed, exhaling fumes as her mind raced and her hips swirled to a pulsing reggae beat in her head.

Later she was so high, a man she met through one of her

drug relations easily forced her into the bathroom. In no time, Ms. Harvey's panties were off and she got busy, giving it up. They fucked until Ms. Harvey was left squatting, immobilized on the toilet seat. She was completely unaware of time. After urinating, she stumbled off the seat. Her legs were weak and her mind was moving slow. She stood on shaky legs, examining a dismal expression in the bathroom mirror. She had to get away, quickly. Ms. Harvey fixed her clothes ran out the bar and hastily made tracks to her apartment.

Inside the familiar littered haunts, she stood in front of her bathroom mirror. Ms. Harvey wiped away her tears. Shame clouded her thoughts. Her smile was twisted when she thought about the graduation earlier. She was proud to watch her daughter walking across the podium. The feeling of pride overtook her. Suddenly, as if struck by a blast of energy, she jumped and raced out the bathroom.

Ms. Harvey ran to the closet and removed her daughter's graduation gown. She put it on. It swallowed her emaciated frame. She placed the hat and tassels across her face and walked back and forth, pretending to receive her diploma. Then a slow realization hit her hard. She'd cheated. The thought bowled her over onto the sofa. Her stare became fixed on the television. Coco must not find out, she thought. Ms. Harvey jumped up, stripped and got in the shower. She scrubbed herself and then rushed to fix her hair.

Coco always up in my business. I gotta clean up real good. Her thoughts put haste to her actions as she started putting furniture and pillows back in place. Ms. Harvey wandered about the apartment, brushing the furniture off. I need some rest, she thought, picking up the pipe and turning the lighter on high. She puffed hard, sucking on the stem in her quietness.

Ms. Harvey plopped down on the sofa and picked up the remote control. She was about to turn on the television when the ringing phone startled her. She stared blankly at the instrument. Perspiration formed on her brow and her lips went dry. The ringing continued louder. What if it's Coco? The thought was stuck in her head, echoing loudly like a broken record.

Licking her dried lips, she watched wide-eyed as her heart pounded and the phone continued ringing loudly.

"Hello…" she breathed, nervously cradling the phone too close to the side of her face.

In an attempt to hear better what was being said, Ms. Harvey adjusted the instrument. When she heard the screaming on the other end, Ms. Harvey became anxious.

"Hello. Hello. Who is this? Slow down and talk…"

Ms. Harvey held her breath and fearfully listened to the caller. After a few minutes, the phone slipped from her grip. Her body crumpled to the floor. She was staring at the ceiling and her head was shaking side to side. Ms. Harvey opened her mouth but no sound came. Her lips were ashy-gray and dry. Ms Harvey pulled her hair and kicked her legs then stared off as if hypnotized by a beam of light. She finally let out a loud, blood-curdling, guttural wail.

"What did she say?" Deedee asked anxiously.

"I don't know but I don't think she took it very well," Josephine answered, staring at the cellphone in her hand.

Deedee lit another cigarette and they smoked while waiting outside the hospital.

"Do you think Coco's gonna pull through this one, Dee?"

"You know her better than me. I mean you've known her longer and..." Deedee sucked on the cigarette and passed it to Josephine. "One thing I know for sure, she's a powerful sister and a real fighter."

"Yeah, I know. Coco was a… is a great sister," Josephine said.

"I don't know why he had it in for Coco so much."

"Crazy ass, he was trying to kill everyone he came in contact with."

"One thing I'm happy about is he's dead. Eric killed that nigga's ass fer sure," Josephine said.

"My uncle didn't kill him. The detective did," Deedee said immediately.

"I was ducking and running to see what happened to Coco. I didn't know it was the detective who shot his ass. How Eric wind up with the gun in his hand?" Josephine asked.

"The detective gave it to him after he shot Lil' Long."

"Why'd he do that?"

"I don't know. I know my uncle did not shoot anyone."

"You sure it wasn't Eric? The detective took him—"

"I am sure. I saw the whole thing. He's completely innocent,"

Deedee said emphatically.

"My bad. I just thought it was him that's all. I was busy trying to help Coco," Josephine said.

"We better get our stories right. You know the police is gonna be questioning us next," Deedee warned.

"Yeah, I'll say what you told me. You ain't gotta worry 'bout me saying a thing. It's about whether or not Coco's gonna live, right?"

"Yeah, that's what's it's all about," Deedee said. The emotion running through her mind made her sound even more concerned.

"Shit man, I still haven't gotten over losing Dani. I can't lose Coco too…" Josephine's voice trailed and she started crying.

"Yeah, how could anyone forget Dani?" Deedee asked, her mind drifting.

Coco, Danielle and Josephine were all gifted singers and dancers. Coco was special. She was tough but had opened up and shared more with Deedee than any of the other girls. Ever since they met on that ominous night outside the club, their friendship had blossomed to incredible heights.

Da Crew was Danielle—rich, spoiled, sexy beautiful and talented. Josephine was coy and smart. Her dad was a lawyer and her mother a doctor. They kept her under strict control. Being a part of da Crew was her escape. She used to be shy but now she was more outgoing. Josephine, like Danielle, used to use sex and her charm to entrance the man of her interest.

Deedee was aware of Josephine's attraction to her uncle. Danielle would've been flirtatious. She was that way, loose and selfish because she despised sharing the limelight with anyone. Until her death, it was all about Danielle. Deedee stared at Josephine, wondering if Danielle was now living on in Josephine. They hugged and tears flowed.

CHAPTER 2

Detective Kowalski was profusely perspiring, pacing back and forth. His swagger slowed and he rubbed his nose, thinking. The detective wanted to wrap this case up fast.

"Your protections are all gone. Your mob associates were all wiped out. Now level with me! Are you leading a criminal enterprise?" he asked, staring at Eric's nonchalant face. "Am I right? You took care of Maruichi and his boys so you can be a drug kingpin?"

"What the hell are you talking 'bout, man?" Eric snorted.

Kowalski was in the hunt for a suspect and possibly a promotion if he could crack this case open. Eric sat at a desk in the detective's office, his arms folded. He watched as the detective paced in front of him.

Eric was contemplating his next move and glanced at

the presidential Rolex on his wrist. It was five after eight in the morning. His lawyers would arrive soon to get him out of this jam. Having already spent six hours being interrogated by the police, Eric was a little frustrated, but in control.

"Look dick, I ain't stupid so why don't we cut the fun and games. You've got nothing on me. I don't have to say anything until my lawyers walk up in here. Then I'm out. You understand, don't you?" Eric was tired and his voice sounded strained.

"Don't forget, I got a weapon used in the commission of a crime with your prints all over it."

"That's bullshit! I got witnesses. I didn't commit any crimes, dick. My lawyer walks up in here, I walk out. That's what's up!"

"You fucking screwball, you're not going anywhere. This is your gun and it was used in killing a man."

Detective Kowalski discharged the magazine and slammed a black Glock 37 on the desk. The sound of the weapon making contact with the empty desk reverberated through the tiny office. Eric was unshaken but Kowalski's breath was coming fast. He leaned closer and yelled.

"I could make it real bad for you if you don't cooperate!"

Kowalski's tone was menacing but Eric remained unfazed. He folded his arms and smirked at the sweating detective.

"Oh yeah, that's your story, dick. I ain't gotta say no more. My lawyer will be here soon and you're going to have to let me go. Stop the games. You're trying to plant that on me. You and I know it's not working."

Kowalski stared at Eric and shook his head. The brass would back him if he could break the case open. He needed something corroborating. Detective Kowalski thought for a minute. An officer walked into the room and handed Kowalski a note.

"I'm saying this now Ascot. It's cheaper for you to play ball with us," Kowalski warned and stared at the piece of paper.

Then he smiled.

"It seems like your man Lil' Long was planning ahead. He'll be haunting you even in death." Kowalski stood and watched Eric's reaction.

Eric stared at the smiling detective, wondering what was written on the piece of paper.

"What do you mean, dick?"

"Here, read this for yourself," Kowalski said, shoving the note at Eric.

Eric hesitated but took the note. His face contorted when he saw his name and beneath it the (800) BODY-HIT grim reaper signature. Blood rushed to his head, making him woozy. Eric steadied himself and turned the note over as if expecting something other than the dollar amount. He held the paper as if he was weighing it in his hand.

"I mean, your friend, or should I say ex-friend, put out a flat one hundred grand on your head." Kowalski laughed, snapping his fingers like he was rolling dice. "How'd you like that turn of events, huh? Just when you thought you were home free. Now you're gonna have to be looking over your shoulders all the time." The detective paused and snickered. "Now, do you want to cooperate? Remember your good friend, Busta had been marked for such a hit, before you answer. Busta told us a few things about your arrangement before his brain was blown out."

Eric didn't know what to say. He shrugged his shoulders, grabbed his chin and rubbed the stubble on his face. Busta would never snitch. Lil' Long had killed him, he was sure, but Eric didn't know why. Busta stayed connected to the street and had beef with a lot of people.

The detective reached into his bag of tricks and placed a ring on the desk. Eric's mind froze for a beat. He stared at the familiar canary yellow diamond on the ring Busta used to wear on his right pinky finger.

It was as if the detective had found the right bullet for the empty gun on the desk. He smiled wryly when he saw Eric's brow wrinkled and a notable grimace clouding his expression. Eric was pondering all his options. The number one priority was to get out and make sure his niece was okay. Second he needed added security. Eric summed it up in his mind. He looked at the detective sweating him through a heated stare.

"Cooperate…? C'mon man, I already told you I don't know anything. You're barking up the wrong tree!"

"Now you're sounding like Eric Ascot, Mr. Big Time Music Producer, but you're going down one way or the other. There are people out there who killed my partner and I wanna know why and I wanna know it quickly. You can start by telling us all about how you and Busta conspired to murder four people."

Eric looked at the notepaper again and then at the detective. This was a trick to get him to talk. He shoved the note at the befuddled detective.

"When my legal team gets here, you're gonna have to release me, dick. You and I know none of the things you're saying is true. You're just trying to shake me down for info I know nothing about. Do us both a favor and fall back. You've kept me here too long already, wasting my fucking time."

"Yeah, you're gonna probably get your release. But I'm telling you, you're a slime ball and you'll be back crawling and begging once those bullets start coming at you. The bullet only nicked you this time. Next time you might not be so lucky."

"There isn't going to be a next time," Eric said.

"They're all dead, Eric. Busta, Maruichi and his boys, we're all you've got left. Come straight and we can work out a deal," the detective offered.

"Deal? You cannot be serious?"

"We'll see. You're brave now. Next time you won't be able to fucking make up a song about it because you'll be a dead cocksucker!" Kowalski screamed in Eric's face.

"Yeah, I don't care about your theories," Eric said.

"I'm gonna give them to you anyhow," Kowalski said, leaning closer. "You and your former friend, Busta, have been in contact with a hit squad, an organization which goes by some kind of code. Now we can prove the organization is responsible in the killing of at least four police officers and several civilians on someone's orders. Your involvement has already been determined. Now you can tell us who gave the orders for those people to die. Give me names and some reasons why these people were murdered!"

The detective's bellowing didn't rattle Eric, who calmly adjusted the yellow diamond cuff links on his Gucci shirt.

"I was shot," he said. "You've had me cooped up in this

office all morning trying to get me to answer questions on shit I don't know about. I guess you don't know when to quit, huh?" Eric was looking at the gun.

"Why did he want you dead?"

"Maybe he was a disgruntled fan. He didn't like my last song. I don't know. Maybe you know dick."

The detective was rattled and grabbed Eric by his shirt collar. Eric rose to his feet as the detective continued shaking him.

"He may have missed that time you sonofabitch! There'll be other chances to prove just how tough you are!" Kowalski screamed.

Two uniform officers came busting through the door. They fought and struggled to get the detective off Eric. During the commotion, Eric was hit twice in the face before they finally dragged the irate Kowalski away.

"You better cut a deal right now. The price on your head guarantees you'll be back begging for our help," Kowalski shouted as he was pulled out the office. "You're gonna be begging—"

"Muthafucka get outta my face," Eric muttered while examining his torn shirt. A couple minutes later, a uniformed officer returned. "That muthafucka must be crazy," Eric said. looking at his injured arm. \Another officer approached him.

"They giving you a hard time?" the officer asked.

"This shirt must be offensive," he sighed, shaking his head.

"You can leave. Your lawyers have bailed you out," he said.

Eric got up and adjusted his clothes. The chief stepped in front of him, looking him up and down.

"I don't like your kind. You rap millionaires wearing your expensive clothes trying to pass yourselves off as decent people…"

"I'm not a rap millionaire, I'm a music producer I do all types of—"

"Whatever you are, all the hip-hop-pity-shit makes no difference to me. At the end of the day, you're still a criminal so you better be prepared to pay them high price lawyers a lot of damn money. You can guarantee one thing. We will get you. Go on back to your studio and put it in a damn song, Mr. Music Producer."

He was mean-grilling so close to Eric that blobs of spit crashed into his face. Eric pulled out a silk handkerchief and wiped his face.

"You made your point," Eric said before walking out the office.

Kowalski, the chief and his superiors were staring at him as if he were a prize. They watched Eric strut to the front desk and shake hands with his lawyer.

"We need constant surveillance on him. He's a tough guy with a soft heart. Let's find where he's slipping and then let's pounce. Give him a lot of attention, I want wiretaps to go over his telephone records. He's connected somehow. Find me something so I can nail the nigga to the wall," the chief ordered. "We've got to wrap this case and very soon. We need the murderer caught. The department already lost a couple of good men in this one. We can't afford to drag this one too long, especially you Kowalski.

He helped to kill your partner. Now get on your jobs!" the chief ordered.

A group of detectives huddled and as Eric walked by, they nodded and dispersed. Eric stood at the front desk and conferring for a few minutes with his attorney. They walked away still in conversation.

"Are you alright, Eric? Everything is alright. But apparently someone from their side notified the media. The news hounds are waiting outside. I'll handle them if you want me to."

"I want you to handle them. I'll... I'll..." Eric was worn out.

His attorney turned and looked at the precinct commander, smiled and continued walking. Outside flashbulbs went off and reporters bumrushed the pair. Eric shook off the early morning sluggishness he felt and gave a good performance with a smile. Pictures were taken and the attorney started answering questions. Eric kept walking but was unable to avoid the ugly glare of the cameras and queries.

"How was your stay Mr. Ascot?" a paparazzo asked.

"How'd you like to be cooped up in a police precinct answering questions all night without being charged? And to make matters worse, I was the victim of a crime. Despite all that provocation, I'm doing real well. My songs are popping off the charts and I'm about to embark on a new project…"

"Why were you in taken in?"

"I don't know. Maybe the detective is a strong advocate for censorship of my music."

"What was the charge?"

"No charges have been leveled at Mr. Ascot at this time

or any other time. An apparent robbery attempt was made earlier today…" the attorney started.

Eric slipped past the crowd, blinking and reaching for his shades, when he spotted someone who looked like Sophia. He stared and he felt a rush of adrenalin when he realized it was indeed his ex-fiancée.

"Well, I see you've not lost all your usual charisma, Mr. Ascot," Sophia said, smiling.

"Sophia, what the hell are you doing here?"

"Don't worry. At the behest of my boss, I'm here to get your signature on some of Busta's paperwork. Otherwise, I would not come and see you. This is strictly business!"

The impatience in her tone drew a cautious stare from Eric. Sophia was his fiancée but after Busta was killed, he had to sure up security. Eric did so with the help of the Maruichi brothers. They were linked to organized crime. Citing fear for her life and reputation, Sophia walked away. Eric pulled up his Marc Jacobs goggles, wrapping his eyes while looking searchingly in hers. The love was there but she had lost respect for his ways. He smiled easily.

"Business, huh?" he asked.

"Yes Eric, business. I don't want to know why you're in and out of jail."

"I've been held and interrogated by the police and you come—"

"I'm not interested in your ghetto point of view," Sophia said, raising her hand.

"I see you haven't lost the nasty little attitude of yours.

Do you want to discuss this business here, or should we go somewhere else where you can rake me over the fire in private?" Eric asked, looking around for a cab.

"I've got the firm's chauffeur if you want to go somewhere," Sophia said, turning away from Eric. His eyes checked her out from head to toe. He licked his lips and felt the lump in his throat.

"Good. Give me a ride cross town," he said with his eyes riveted on her backside.

"What's across town?"

"I have to get Deedee," Eric said casually.

"Oh, she doesn't have a ride?"

"Yes but she's at St Vincent's with her—"

"What? What is she doing at the hospital…?" Sophia stared at Eric anxiously.

"I'll tell you about it on the way there."

"No,. Tell me now. What happened to Deedee?" Sophia asked, grabbing Eric's arm. "I'm sorry, but you just can't say something like that, especially about Deedee, and walk away. I know she was…"

"It's not Deedee. It's Coco. She was shot last night."

"What? Coco? You mean... Coco... we saw her, I saw her performing and... Oh my God! Is she dead…?"

"She's holding on," Eric said.

Sophia waved for the car and a black Cadillac stretch pulled over to stop in front of them.

"What happened?"

"Let go of my arm and I'll tell you about it on the way."

Sophia freed his arm and he held the door. Getting into

the car, she wobbled and Eric steadied her.

"Thank you," she said and nervously sat. "Tell me what happened, Eric."

CHAPTER 3

"Oh shit. It was on when 'em damn Chinese bitches got up in there, Kim. The bitches sprayed the whole place and not one single shot touch me or my son. Thank you God," Tina said, making the sign of the cross across her chest. "Cuz, if they would've hit me or Junior it would really be on."

Tina hugged herself and puffed hard on the cigarette. Under the cold scrutiny of Kim, she snuffed out the rest of the cigarette into an ashtray. They were sitting in Kim's destroyed two-bedroom apartment. Tina was there after leaving her son at her parents' apartment. Kim shook her head and stared at Tina with pity.

"Bitch, shut the fuck up! If them Chinos would've shot you, it be over. That's all there is to it—"

"Why you gonna say it like that, Kim? I wasn't part of

Nesto's mix up. He the one they were after. I mean I had no—"

"Bitch, don't you know I know? Those same muthafuckas roll up in this crib on my ass. They killed Carlos, right out there in the hallway. That shit had the police all up in here. Lucky thing Roshawn was with me or else... Shit! You talking bout a scared-ass bitch. I went straight to church."

"Kim, *you* went to church? See, now I know anything is possible."

"Don't talk like I don't be going? I goes to church. Last Easter I went to church."

"Easter? That was months ago."

"Okay, but when was the last time you went to church?"

"Don't start acting and talking like you a regular and all that. If it wasn't on account of Carlos being in here up that coochie your ass would never have gone again until next Easter."

"Nah, I would've gone on Thanksgiving and Christmas," Kim said.

"What? You the type that be going only on holidays?"

"Damn Skippy, and special occasions too, like when your boy and his friends goes and steals shit that's not theirs. I knew it."

"You know what?"

"I knew Ernesto was nothing but trouble. Can't say I never told you. And what you mean up in my coochie?"

"Ha, ha," Tina snickered. "I thought you didn't hear. But your ass wasn't telling me nothing like that, okay. You were telling me to give him one more chance—"

"Me? I wasn't saying no shit like that," Kim countered. Her

tone was an octave higher. "Your crotch was on fire as soon as you saw the no good bastard. Your ass didn't even remember who your real friends was. If those bitches hadn't put the fear of God in your ass, you'd still be home cooking damn rice and beans for the lazy ass nigga."

"Pipe down, Kim. You're gonna burst a damn blood vessel."

"You should've told them Chinese bitches with the Uzi's or whatever machine guns those was to pipe down. I bet you never say shit to them, huh?"

"No-muthafucking-way-Jose was I opening my fucking mouth. Shit, I was in a heller shock. I couldn't even speak if I wanted to, not one damn word..." Tina's voice trailed and her eyes wandered around Kim's ruined living room.

"So why do you think it's okay for you to come up in here and shoot your mouth off then tell me to pipe down? Answer that one, bitch."

"I'm saying be easy with your mouth, bitch. You gonna wake up your own son."

"You leave Roshawn outta this, alright? Lucky thing he's able to sleep after all this horror.

"Where's he at?"

"In his bed safely sleeping. Damn! Look at my fucking place. It's a total wreck. Ugh...who's gonna replace my shit after them two Chinese bitches ransacked and fucked up my damn place!"

"You don't have to tell me. They went through my place and pointed them same guns at me, Kim. I swear to God, I pissed right there," Tina said, making the sign of the cross again. "I was trembling the whole time."

"Bitch you should've been shook. They had all rights to be up in your place. He was your baby-daddy and he lives with you. I know Nesto done stole their ice and shit."

"Carlos was involved too. You know that's why they came here, Kim."

"And his ass was only visiting. They came up in here wearing motorcycle helmets and all. They just started shooting as soon as they saw Carlos. I was scared shitless. It's your fault why I was fucking with Carlos' pimp ass. He had too many women. He wasn't staying here and that's why they shouldn't have shoot up at my damn place. Just look at it now," Kim said, waving her arm around.

Both glanced around the wrecked apartment. The sofa was ripped and flipped over and pillows littered the apartment. CD cases were strewn all over.

"It's you and your man's, I mean ex's fault why they fucked up my place. I was an innocent bystander to this. You're gonna have to help me clean this place up."

"Damn girl! Let me at least mourn his death. I may have to leave town and all."

"Girl please, not over Nesto?"

"I mean…"

"Tina you know the nigga got right back into things as soon as he came home from jail. Him and his boys robbed da wrong fucking people. How I got dragged in some shit where my place becomes people's damn shooting gallery and bitches running up in my muthafucking crib…?"

"Look, I heard your bellyaching. Alright already. I'll do more than help you clean up. You just remember who was there for you when your baby father was shot."

"Oh girl please. You leave Deja outta this one. Don't try to play no sympathy card now!" Kim shouted. "Thank God he's dead. I mean it like they can't blame this one on him. You know all Nesto's boys are snitches and they'd try to pin this on him."

She stared at Tina and saw the fear still in her eyes. They had been friends since junior high. Kim and Tina had had a horrible experience. They faced the wrath of an execution team, known as the Cali6, who were armed with orders to kill. Tina witnessed Nesto being shot down like an animal. Kim was with Carlos when he was gunned down. She feared they would turn their guns on her but they didn't. Instead they quickly rummaged around her one bedroom apartment and disappeared as fast as they came. Kim hugged Tina.

"Don't get too emotional about Nesto. He was up to no good."

"Kim, that was some crazy shit," she whispered.

"Was it? Oh God, I'll never forget it. I didn't even know nothing. They were looking for ice," Kim said. "What the fuck I know 'bout some ice…?"

She glanced suspiciously at Tina like old friends who know each other well do. The pressure was on and Tina was reluctant to respond. She walked to where she'd placed her black Campo style handbag and played with the braided straps.

Kim watched, looking at her best friend wringing her

hands, anxious to say something.

"Kim I know sump'n about their ice. I'm trying to tell you."

"Don't tell me nothing. I don't wanna hear anything about it. I don't wanna be involved in anything—"

"I kept a chunk," Tina said with a smile that immediately brought a painful grimace on Kim's mug.

"What?" Kim's voice boomed. She wore a stunned expression. "Now why the fuck did you tell me that. I don't wanna fucking know nothing. You feel me? I don't wanna be mixed up in this scheme…"

Kim's voice trailed and her mouth dropped open when Tina pulled out the gleaming, huge rock. The small egg-sized jewel glistened brightly in the morning's sunlight. Tina held it up and they stared awestruck at the stone's size and clarity.

"Woooooooow," Kim said. She involuntarily whistled while carrying a wide-eyed expression. "That is some big ass piece of rock. Someone is gonna get killed."

They were startled by the ringing doorbell. Both gazed at the door as if they were hypnotized. "Put… put the shit back where it came from and don't leave that big ass diamond anywhere in my apartment. I don't want them two Chinese bitches coming back and shooting me and my son," Kim said, walking slowly to the door, all the while keeping her eyes on Tina.

"Oh Tina, put that shit away. Hide it, please! It's the muthafucking super snooping detective you fucked," Kim said, looking at Tina after peering through the peephole. "It's the police, bitch!" she said when the doorbell rang again.

Tina was moving too slow for her and Kim started violently

waving her arms. Tina looked at her perplexed. Kim ran over to where Tina stood and shook her. "I don't want nothin' else going off up in here. Put that shit away," she whispered, hurrying back to the door. "I don't want anymore problems up in here." Kim then opened the door.

The detective walked in wearing a smile and looking nattily dressed in a khaki colored suit and white shirt.

"Good morning ladies," he said. His smile slowly changed to a smirk as he pulled out his shield.

"Hi detective. How're you doing?" Kim smiled.

He walked over and gently grabbed Tina close to him.

"Y'all need to go get a room somewhere," Kim said with a smile that wasn't very convincing.

"I thought I'd find you here," Detective Kowalski said. "What you got hiding in this expensive handbag of yours?"

Kim felt a shudder, for she was anxious that Kowalski may have seen the diamond.

"Looks like this place has been through a storm," Kowalski observed.

He put the bag down and Kim's heart beat dropped. She sashayed over and planted herself between the handbag and Kowalski. Tina winked at her and wiggled her ass in front of Kowalski, averting his attention. He followed her to where the sofa stood flipped over. Kim picked up the bag and took it to her bedroom. She returned to see Kowalski pawing at Tina's body.

"Hey, hey, what's the rush? Y'all acting like horn-toads. You get it whenever you can, huh?"

"He's just happy to see me," Tina said with a grin.

"You and him need to take y'alls happiness elsewhere," Kim said wiping her hands across her neck. "Dead that shit! Go with the detective to brunch or sump'n. And don't forget your bag. I put it in the bedroom."

"I'm too tired to eat. I'm dead ass if I get sump'n to eat. I'll fall out and sleep right there," Tina said, spinning her colorfully manicured nail in the air. "I'm dead ass."

"Well, I gotta clean up all this mess right now."

"I'll help you," Tina said quickly.

"Now wait up. Before you ladies get busy with cleaning up the mess. The chief would like to talk to you."

"Tell your boss, the chief or whoever to give us a call and set up an appointment," Tina said.

"I don't know—" the detective started.

"You don't understand—" Kim quickly cut the detective off.

"I understand alright, but I can't go anywhere right now. My son is sleeping and he's been through hell. I just want him to get a little more rest."

"They want to see you now and you can take your son," the detective ordered.

Kim gave him an evil stare and was about to jump all over him but Tina intervened.

"Hey, you know what? Let's go down and see what the chief has to say. You can drop Roshawn off at my mother's and she'll—"

"How you gonna be taking on biz for your mother like that? What if she got sump'n else to do and shit."

"Kim, she's taking care of Junior. She'll do the same for Roshawn," Tina assured her.

Kim looked at her for a beat then glanced back at the detective.

"Can I at least get dressed?" she asked, sashaying with a frown.

"Sure, just don't take all day. The chief doesn't like to be kept waiting," Kowalski smiled, patting Kim's rotund ass.

"Okay, watch it now. Don't let me have to go that sexual harassment route," she said, smiling at Kowalski.

"Don't you ever say those words again to me!"

Kim was startled and stared at the scowl on the detective's face. It slowly dawned on her that the fury in his voice was real. He had taken her seriously. There was a misunderstanding.

"I'm sorry I didn't mean to—"

Kowalski was furious. He grabbed her shoulders and shook her violently. Kim's fright showed in the white of her eyes. She gasped for breath.

"If you even hint at this again black bitch, I'll put my foot so far up your fat-ass-"

"Hey be easy with my friend," Tina interrupted, grabbing onto Kowalski's arm. "I thought we had an appointment with your boss. You're gonna shake the shit outta her. Let her go so she can go change. Mike, please let her go."

Kowalski's body slowly relaxed and he calmed down. He let out a loud sigh as Kim slipped away from his grip. The detective pulled Tina close and kissed her hard.

"Now where were we?" he asked.

"Huh uh…" she fumbled for an answer.

CHAPTER 4

They stood outside the hospital together, Josephine's lips lazily clinging to a cigarette while peeking beneath her Gucci frames. Deedee's wary eyes were hidden behind shades styled by Dolce and Gabanna. She was watching for any signs of her uncle's return. Her mind was on Coco,. Deedee shifted her weight from one hip to the next. She glanced at the bodyguard sitting and waiting for any word from her uncle. Eric had instructed him to stay with the girls.

"Hey Deedee. Eric's on his way," he shouted after closing his cellphone.

"Thanks Big C," Deedee said perking up.

"It's about time them cops let him go," Josephine said, inhaling so hard on the cigarette that her veins were bulging.

Deedee turned to look at her and then back to the busy

early morning traffic of the city street. A black stretch rolled to a stop and the rear window came down.

"Hi Dee."

"Sophia! Oh my. Where did you come from?" Deedee smiled.

Josephine smiled and her heart lifted when she saw Eric exiting the limousine. She smiled sheepishly at Eric and made a weak attempt at hugging him. His response seemed force and uncomfortable. Quickly, he dashed by her outstretched arms and hurried over to where Deedee stood flabbergasted. He hugged his niece and they walked closer to the limo. Josephine felt the rejection and made a promise to check him on his behavior later when they were in private.

She strolled slowly behind them, caught up in her thoughts. An internal alarm was triggered when she recognized that Sophia had traveled with him in the limo. Josephine quickened her pace and quickly caught up with Deedee and Eric as a jolt of jealousy coursed through her. Josephine stood back as they spoke.

"Hi uncle," Dee said.

"Dee, are you okay? Sorry to leave you waiting."

"It's okay. I'm alright."

"Heard anything yet?"

"They told us only family members could see her. I don't know what's up. They refused to talk to us. So we called her mother and I don't know what happened,"

"You don't know but that woman is likely drunk or cracked-out or both," Josephine said, cutting Deedee off.

"Maybe, we don't know for sure," Deedee added.

"I called her and she sounded like something was up. She was sounding quite suspect to me," Josephine said.

After speaking with the driver, Sophia got out of the stretch and joined them. Deedee gave her a long embrace and Josephine seemed confused as to whether to join them. Finally she entered the hug-fest. Her reluctance drew Eric's attention.

After a few nervous heartbeats, the loud siren of an ambulance broke up their embrace.

Sophia broke free. She was tearing when she said, "I think I can get some information on her. What's her full name?" she asked remembering that working with the D.A. had given her certain privileges.

"Coco Harvey," Josephine spat, thinking about how Eric had spurned her.

"You guys stay in the lounge. Let me go check on her," Sophia said and walked away.

They followed her into the hospital. Both girls sat and Eric continued standing for a moment, then he went after Sophia.

"Can I go with you as your assistant or something?"

"Something? No, I'll do just fine," Sophia said and left Eric standing in awe.

He watched her curves. Eric was still enchanted by Sophia's moves. He smiled, shaking his head, and walked back to the waiting area. The look on his niece's face brought him back to the reality of it all. He sat next to Deedee with his arm about her shoulder, completely ignoring the green-eyed glare Josephine wore. She quietly seethed.

Josephine stood with as much movement as possible and

sashayed over to the vending machine. She bent over. In tight Prada jeans and Manolo four-inch heels, the roundness of her ass was on display. She checked her wallet and with an exaggerated swing of her hips, Josephine slowly strutted back to where Eric sat.

"Do yer have chinge fer a ten spot?" Josephine smiled with a mock southern drawl.

Eric reached into his pocket and fished out a couple dollars and some change. Josephine allowed the quarters to fall in his lap. She grabbed his crotch while retrieving them. All the time Deedee pretended to be asleep in her uncle's arm.

"Do you want something from the machine?" Josephine smiled.

"Nah, I'm good," Eric lazily replied.

"I'll get you something that you won't be able to resist."

He eyed Josephine, who strutted back to the vending machine. She selected sweet and sour candy and a chocolate bar. He watched her sucking on the chocolate bar. She tossed him the candy.

"This is what I want to do to you," she said.

Eric was in a daze between sleep and exhaustion. He didn't make an attempt to catch the candy and the packet fell to the floor.

"Oops…my bad," Josephine said and raced over. In retrieving the candy she rubbed Eric's crotch and sat in his lap.

So involved was she in caressing Eric's face, no one saw Sophia walk into the waiting area. She walked over to where they were.

"Alright, I hate to break up this nice family setting but I've got to get to work," Sophia said after waiting a couple of stressful beats.

Eric jumped up so quickly Josephine almost fell from his lap. Deedee opened her eyes, hoping for the best.

"What's going on?" Deedee asked. "Did you see her?"

"No, but I spoke in length to the doctor caring for her."

"Really, what did he say?" Josephine asked.

"Well, let's see, the doctor's name is and she's very capable dealing with trauma cases such as Coco's. The best possible news is Coco isn't dead. The doctor thinks she's been through the worse but she has ways to go before making a complete recovery."

A collective sigh of relief was released. Sophia looked at the group and waited as they digested everything she had to say.

"Are there any bad news?" Josephine asked sheepishly

"I'm not a medical expert so I'm gonna try to repeat what the doctor told me. Ah… because of the trauma directly to her head there was an increase of cerebrospinal fluid pressure by the ventricles of her brain—"

"I don't understand," Josephine said impatiently.

"Yeah, what does all this mean?" Deedee asked.

Sophia paused and her tears came. She dried her eyes with a tissue before she continued.

"Coco can't see right now. She's blind," she said.

The air seemed to have been swept away with the wail from Deedee's lips.

"No-o-o..." she moaned as if in pain. She appeared faint.

Eric looked confused. He couldn't believe what was coming out of Sophia's mouth.

"Are you sure...are you for sure...?" he asked looking dumbfounded.

"I'm sure I'm repeating exactly what the doctor told me," Sophia said with her eyebrow raised. "She will pull through, but she's still a long way off."

"What are her chances to recover and see again?" Josephine asked.

"I don't really know, Josephine. But you guys can pray and start visiting her as soon as she comes out of intensive care. They have to run some tests on her to determine exactly what's going on inside her brain. Her recovery will be up to Coco," Sophia said.

Deedee was crying and Josephine hugged her. "Coco is tough, she'll get through this. When the going gets rough, the tough gets going," Josephine said, trying to sound confident.

"I guess they will contact us..."

"I gave them my cell and office numbers. They'll call as soon as changes develop and I'll pass the news on to you guys. There is a question about her mother's whereabouts."

"Yeah, we called her at home because the nurse told us to let her know Coco was in the hospital and she had to come down and sign papers," Deedee said.

"And what happened?" Sophia asked.

"I spoke to her and... don't know. Maybe she was high or

sump'n," Josephine said. "I called back and the phone was either busy or off the hook."

"Coco and her mother are still living uptown, right?" Sophia asked.

"Yep, in the same Malcolm X projects," Josephine said.

"Let's at least make an attempt to contact her mother in person," Sophia suggested. "I'll have to call my office to let them know I'll be delayed, but I think I can spare the time."

They walked out the hospital. The news wasn't all bad, Deedee thought, holding Sophia's arm. Eric had his arm around his niece. Josephine walked alone for a moment then she held onto Deedee's arm. The girls and Eric were exhausted but hopes were raised. Sophia led the way to the waiting limousine dialing on her Blackberry.

"Uptown, ah, one hundred and tenth street and Lenox, please," Sophia said hanging up and they were all seated inside the limousine.

After the short ride, they entered the building and stood in the lobby waiting for the elevator. There were no other residents standing around. Eric, Sophia, Deedee and Josephine stood there pressing buttons on the elevator door for a couple of minutes.

"The elevator is out of order," someone said going by.

"I should've known better. Coco always says it's never working. Let's take the stairs," Josephine said.

"Lead the way," Eric said, holding Sophia and Deedee.

Josephine went in front and the others followed her to the stairwell.

"The apartment is on the third floor," she said, climbing

the stairs.

"Pew, this place stinks," Sophia said, holding her nose.

"Watch out for the gigantic rats," Josephine cautioned.

"Oh please, Josephine is over exaggerating things," Deedee deadpanned.

"I think she's right, Dee. I just saw a big one ran back there on the second floor," Eric said and Sophia shrieked. She wound up in Eric's arm. Still scared of rats, Eric thought and smiled. Sophia hugged him all the way up the stairs.

On the third floor, Josephine found the door and knocked on it while the others waited. She rang the doorbell and strutted back and forth impatiently. Josephine eyed Eric's closeness with Sophia and Deedee. She tried not to mind. Josephine comforted herself with the thought of she and Eric being together real soon.

There was no answer. The others were about to give up and get out of the hallway. Josephine had other ideas. She took her heels off and used them to bang loudly on the door.

"C'mon, Jo," Eric said. "She might not be—"

"Listen, someone's up."

The rumblings from inside grew louder. It sounded like the person was dragging their feet in the direction of the door.

"Who da fuck is at my door this early? Its Saturday. Can a tired bitch sleep in? If it's the Jehovah Witness people, I done took some magazines…"

The door opened and Ms. Harvey stood wide eyed with surprise. Her lips were ashy and dry. Her disheveled appearance was a shock to all. Deedee jumped with surprise at the state of Coco's mother.

"Ah… I'm sorry, you know 'em Jehovah's Witness always banging loud on your door especially on a Saturday." Ms. Harvey smiled uneasily. She kept fidgeting with her hair. It would take a stylist all day to set it right but Ms. Harvey seemed determined to fix it then and there. "Coco isn't here. She hanging out with her other friends. You know she got a lot of friends now. I was with some friends at a bar, celebrating her good deeds."

Ms. Harvey broke down and started crying loudly. Her howling had neighbors opening their doors.

"Y'all better come inside. You don't know these—"

"Ms. Harvey, we called you earlier this morning," Josephine said.

"Oh really? Come inside, come inside," Ms. Harvey said, pulling herself together "I thought it was some prank caller. They're so rude calling and hanging up all the time. You can't trust people. I don't call anyone and hang up. I always leave a damn message. It's the right thing to do."

Ms. Harvey drew her red housecoat about her emaciated frame. The visitors were baffled by Ms. Harvery's behavior.

"Everyone with a cellphone think they can call you from anywhere in the world and you can hear them. I can't hear them. My phone is in the house. You can call anywhere and somewhere… cellphone... ah… Coco doesn't have a cellphone so if you want, you're welcome to wait on her. I'm mad at her. She'll come creeping in but I got news for her." Tears began rolling down Ms. Harvey's cheek. Sophia reached out with a Kleenex. The woman seemed dazed and ignored her.. "Coco isn't here. She went out with her other friends. They went clubbing… Come in."

"We know Ms. Harvey," Sophia said as they stepped inside.

It was dark and dingy inside the apartment. A foul odor of burnt plastic greeted them. The place was reeking of burnt plastic and ammonia. A stale, foul odor emanated throughtout. The visitors held their collective breaths.

"Could we just open the shade a lil' sump'n, please?" Josephine asked.

"Yes, please open a window," Sophia requested. "It's a nice day out."

"You can't trust no one. Sometimes I forget to close the window and they come in here—Coco always make sure all the windows and the door are locked. No one is ever gonna sneak up on her." Ms. Harvey was crying and nervously chattering.

Sophia moved closer to her. Deedee and Josephine glanced around the place. Things seemed ordinary except on the center table.

"Ms. Harvey..." Sophia started.

While Eric and Sophia looked around the place, the eyes of Deedee and Josephine followed Ms. Harvey. The woman quickly and cunningly scooped remnants of last night's party, all the time ignoring her company. She quickly walked away to the trash can in the kitchen, dumped the works and then hurried back.

"Sit down and have a seat. She ain't here yet. Y'all might as well get comfy. She bought this sofa, you know? Y'all gonna wait for Coco, right? I can't wait to see her… ooh, she know not to be out so late… all night? Now you know this a little bit too ridiculous," Ms. Harvey said.

The woman slowed down for a bit and Sophia seized the moment as Ms. Harvey sat down.

"Ms. Harvey. Ah… well, Coco, she's in the hospital downtown—"

"Huh, what?" the woman shouted, jumping up. Her housecoat opened, revealing a body withering with years of drug abuse. Her sagging breast waved side to side as she spoke incoherently. "What's Coco doing down in the hospital?" She gathered the red robe at the waist. "I mean, why's Coco downtown, in some hospital? What she doing, huh? That girl done lost her mind. You just wait until she gets up in here," Ms. Harvey ranted.

"Ms Harvey, she—" Sophia said, with tears welling. She reached into her purple Chloe handbag for a Kleenex tissue.

"She was supposed to be celebrating her high school graduation. She did great. She delivered her speech and walked across the stage. I was so proud of my daughter. I went and had a few drinks at the bar with my friends. I had to celebrate but I came back home. She's still not here… oh… Then what the fuck is she doing in a damn hospital downtown?"

Ms. Harvey paused as the words ricocheted slowly off her inebriated mind. She sat down pulling the robe about her. The deranged mother's tiny frame seemed to disappear in the shroud of the fabric. The visitors were speechless and Ms. Harvey let out a loud and long, piercing scream.

"No-o-oooooo… Don't tell me… please don't tell me," she shouted sobbing loudly.

The visitors looked at her in awe. There were no dry eyes in the apartment. Sophia rushed to her aide. She hugged the distraught mother as she spoke to her.

"Ms Harvey, Coco was shot, but she's recovering. The doctors want to talk to you."

"Shot!" she shrieked and started hopping around the place.

The bad news shot her into a fit of hysteria. Eric rushed to hold Sophia because he felt she was in danger of being hit by Ms. Harvey's flailing arms. He moved her out the way just in time. The distraught mother wailed for minutes. Ms. Harvey curled her frail body into a fetal position on the floor, crying like a newborn. With tear-stained face, she glanced hopefully at Eric, Deedee and Josephine in turn. She got up, shook her head and walked away .

"I tried to warn her about all this hanging out but she wouldn't listen," Ms. Harvey said. Then suddenly, she paused. "What the doctor want to see me for? I wasn't with her. I didn't shoot her," Ms. Harvey said, looking around, expecting an answer. Then she chuckled. "They should be out looking for the peoples who shot my daughter. I'm going down there. What hospital she in? I'm going there to give them doctors and everybody sump'n to think about. They just killed Miss Katie, they ain't gonna kill Coco. The first thing you know you get shot and they wanna do heart surgery so they can bill the city. It's all the damn new HMO and healthcare plan. You can't just go to any doctor. You gotta find one inside your health plan and if he's not good then you can't change cause they won't pay.That HMO Miss Katie belonged to wouldn't approve any more treatment for her. And her insurance was up, so they pulled the life-plug on her. Those doctors wanna tell you who can live and who can't. It's the fittest of the fit and the richest of the rich who rules. I'm poor, so I'm gonna get change and go see my daughter. What hospital you say she's at?"

"St. Vincent's," Sophia said.

Ms. Harvey walked away, leaving a heavy, dark haze in the living room. Sophia sniffled still feeling the woman's pain. Eric moved close and hugged her. Immediately, thoughts of his dead brother's wife, who had been missing for over ten years, swam in his head. She was probably lying dead somewhere unknown, Eric mused. She was a victim of an awful crack habit and behaved a lot like Coco's mother. The reason Deedee felt close to Coco dawned on him. It hit him like a ton of bricks. He remembered how Deedee described her mother the last she had seen her.

Denise, his dead brother's wife, had gotten heavily into drugs after his brother's sudden death. She couldn't handle his murder, for he had died in an ambush which remained unsolved. His death had hurt everyone. Deedee told Eric about vividly remembering the last month before her mother, Denise, was carried away by the police and paramedics after stealing to support her burgeoning crack habit. She lost a lot of weight, there were a lot of similarities between her mother's appearance and Coco's mother. Deedee always spoke about the hatred she felt toward her mother.

He had tried to explain but Deedee didn't want to understand. She wouldn't listen. She had quietly changed her name on the school register by forging her mother's signature. She had been Denise D. Ascot, but changed it to Deedee. Deedee despised her mother because of the drug abuse. During the period they lived together, Deedee told him of often wishing for her mother's death. She used to say a special prayer before going to sleep.

"Dear God, I pray you take my mommy back or let her die tonight."

Ten years ago, an ambulance carried her unconscious mother away on a stretcher. Denise had overdosed on crack-cocaine and heroin. Deedee, instead of feeling sadness, felt relieved. She had hoped her mother would never come back. Eric had wanted to please his niece and made all her wishes reality.

Deedee never saw her mother again after the overdose. The young teen would eventually grow to miss her mother. Even though she tried to hide it, Eric knew she wanted to see her mother again, especially after she was raped. She cried for her mother daily. Eric had made a secret deal with Busta to get rid of the embarrassment Deedee'ds mother had caused. Now Busta was dead and he could never go back on it. Eric was the only one alive carrying the enormous weight of the deal with Busta. He had accumulated wealth from the music and entertainment industry and could easily provide financially for his niece, but there was one thing he could never give back to her. It was her mother.

Eric assumed the role of Deedee's father and full-time guardian. In order for Deedee to have a mother again, he made plans to marry Sophia, who used to work for Busta while attending college. But his marital plans didn't work out how he'd planned it. Sophia had backed out because of his involvement with the mob. Yet that was old news. Maybe now Sophia would be willing to reconsider, he thought.

By hanging with Coco, Deedee saw her mother. Eric wanted to help his niece. He glanced at her and she had her eyes closed. His musing was interrupted when Josephine started bawling, attracting everyone's attention. Eric reached out and held her hand. Josephine hugged his shoulder. Deedee's mind was on Coco as she quietly cried and prayed.

"This is crazy, fucking crazy. Too fucking crazy. I told Coco not to hang out. I know what it is to hang out and not get shot. But she's got to be tough..."

They jumped when they heard Ms. Harvey's voice. It trailed and they heard crying. Fifteen minutes later she came out the bedroom. Ms. Harvey was dressed in bright green jeans and red T-shirt. Tears rolled down her cheek as she laced up her multi-colored Reeboks. She raced off into another room and returned with a light green jacket. Ms. Harvey grabbed her handbag and keys. She walked to the door.

"Are y'all gonna wait here? I'm a go check on Coco," she said.

The visitors all looked at her with surprise.

"Why the fuck, are y'all staring at me like that? Is everything alright for me to go see my daughter?" Ms. Harvey asked. "Y'all welcome to stay an all but don't be like my friend, Gladys, always stealing sump'n. Y'all are Coco's friend so y'all can stay but don't steal nothing. I'm warning y'all right now," Ms Harvey said and was about to head out.

"No we're not staying, we're going with you," Sophia said quickly. "As a matter of fact, I've got a car and we can give you a ride downtown."

"Woman, you mad as hell. One, two, three..." Ms. Harvey said, counting each person. "All these people in one car? And look at his size. He got some weight on," she said pointing at Eric. He led the girls walked out the apartment. "And them two, they packing. Them young girls don't stay young too long. It's a conspiracy by the government. They control everything." Ms. Harvey paused and locked the door.

"It's a big limousine," Sophia said.

"That'll work. The elevator doesn't," she said, heading to the stairs. "They fix it one day and the next day it's fucked up. I don't know why they just don't get a new one. I'm sure it could be replaced but the city don't want to spend no money on the poor."

They went down the stairs and Ms. Harvey's ranting went on pause, but she resumed outside.

"Always in the streets, I tried to tell her about hanging out. You know at least five or six people have to be killed before Coco gets the message. She thinks she's invincible. I been telling her it was gonna happen. Man there's too many guns in the wrong hands."

Eric opened the door and everyone got inside. Ms. Harvey's head swiveled, checking out the amenities of the luxury ride.

"Oh shit, this is real big. But can it go fast?"

The others looked at her and tried to hold their smile. Deedee closed her eyes and rested her head against her uncle's shoulder. Josephine sat across, staring at them. Ms. Harvey and Sophia chitchatted like old friends as the car sped downtown.

CHAPTER 5

The unmarked police car with Kim, Roshawn and Tina in the backseat pulled to a stop outside Tina's apartment building. Her mother lived on the second floor and Tina lived on the sixth floor. Tina and Kim got out of the car. Tina knew she would have to convince her mother and made an offer to Kim.

"I'll take Roshawn up to my mother's. You could stay in the car," Tina suggested.

"I'm not staying in that car with that crazy-ass detective," Kim whispered as she and Tina stared at each other.

"Okay, get Roshawn and come on. I gotta put sump'n away," Tina said.

"Hey what's taking you two so long? Let's get things moving along already," Kowalski shouted from inside the car. He was on the radio as Tina and Kim carried Roshawn went into the building.

"I've got our bait," he smiled, watching Kim and Tina's backsides.

They returned five minutes later without Roshawn. Kim and Tina jumped in the back seat and Kowalski sped away.

The limousine carrying Ms. Harvey pulled to a stop outside the hospital. The driver was out the car, holding the door. Sophia, Deedee and Josephine exited the stretch. Eric waited for Ms. Harvey. She seemed to be stalling as she gathered herself.

"After you," Eric said.

Ms. Harvey appeared to scowl and waited a few beats before finally getting out of the luxurious confines. Her steps were shaky and Sophia held her arm. Deedee rushed to her other side, preventing the distraught mother from falling.

Ms. Harvey hobbled with panicky feet up to the entrance of the hospital. She paused at the door and went through a transformation as she entered the lobby.

"Alright, alright," Ms. Harvey said, sounding annoyed.

She pushed Sophia away, who waved off Deedee.

"Where's my daughter?" she demanded.

The receptionist was surprised by the visitor's outburst. She stood with her mouth saying nothing, eyeing Ms. Harvey. Hospital security came rushing in from all directions.

"There are such things as manners. You should—"

Sophia jumped into the fray.

"I'm sorry. This is Ms. Harvey and she's under a tremendous amount of stress since finding out her daughter has been shot and—"

"It doesn't mean she should take her frustration out on everyone else," the receptionist said.

"Again, I apologize for Ms. Harvey. She's been really shaken up by the news," Sophia said, softening the cold, hard stare of a very heated receptionist. She counted to ten before continuing.

"What's your daughter's name?"

"Coco… Coco Harvey," Ms. Harvey answered.

She sheepishly watched the receptionist looking at all the records. After a while the receptionist found the name, picked up the phone and dialed.

"Dr. Gluckmann, is on the third floor," the receptionist said. She turned to Sophia and spoke. You may se the elevator to your left.."

"Thank you," Sophia said and turned to the group.

She hugged Ms. Harvey and walked through the crowded lobby. As soon as they got off the elevator Dr. Gluckmann walked over to them.

"Good morning, are you the mother of—"

"Coco. Where is she, doctor?" Ms. Harvey said cutting the doctor off. "I told her not to be hanging late but she can't listen. Where is she doctor?"

"Well, she's recovering. She's been through a lot—"

"I don't care what she's been through. I wanna see her now. I'm gonna be tightening up things with her..." Ms. Harvey's tears came and her voice trailed.

Sophia hugged her again. Eric addressed the doctor.

"What can we do at this point?" Eric asked.

"Are you her father?"

"No, he ain't my baby-daddy. I'm her mother and you need to be talking to me. Now I want to know, where's my daughter?"

"I'm her manager and these are friends of Coco. We were with her—"

"Y'all were with her. Why none a y'all got bullet wounds? Only Coco, huh...?" Ms. Harvey shouted.

"Her mother has not taken the news well and, ah, we just want to be there for Coco as much as possible. Don't worry about the cost. Do everything you can," Eric said.

"Let's go to my office," the doctor suggested. "Of course there are some roadblocks, but I think her chances for a complete recovery is excellent."

"She's always been living crazy. I knew her luck was gonna run out one day," Ms. Harvey said while crying.

"This was very close, another millimeter and there would've been untold damages to her—"

"Can we see her, doctor? Please let me see my daughter," Ms Harvey requested between tears.

The doctor led them to his office and an assistant helped Ms. Harvey with the task of filling out paperwork. Coco was in intensive care recovering.

"I'm sorry you can't visit her right now but as soon as Dr.

Gluckmann gives the OK, we'll move her someplace where you'll be able to see her on a frequent basis," the assistant said.

"I want to see my daughter. Why can't I see my daughter?" Ms. Harvey yelled.

"I don't know if you're in any condition to see her. She's just out of surgery and she's still asleep. The doctor could authorize you..."

"The doctor? The doctor only care about one thing—my insurance covering his expenses. I don't give a damn! I just wanna see my daughter."

"There are hospital regulations to be followed, Ms. Harvey!" the nurse said and Ms. Harvey took off running down the hall.

"Coco, Coco," she shouted before she was apprehended by security. "Let me go. Y'all got my daughter locked up in here like she was a refugee!" she shouted, screaming and spitting, trying to shake the security.

Soaking wet, she weighed eighty-five pounds. The security was big and muscular, about two-hundred and twenty pounds. It wasn't fair. She was carted off like a rag-doll, arms flailing and legs kicking. The security took the wailing woman inside a room and held her there, awaiting further orders.

The assistant went storming back to the office where Dr. Gluckmann and Eric sat discussing Coco's medical condition.

"She's very adamant about seeing her daughter and refused to fill out the paperwork, Dr. Gluckmann."

"Okay. Don't worry about anything. We can resolve the matter later. Have the nurse attend to her and I'll discuss the situation with her manager," the doctor said, smiling warmly at

Eric. His assistant disappeared.

"How much longer do you think she'll need to stay in the hospital?" Eric asked.

"It's very hard to tell. We're hoping as soon as another week, maybe two. It could be months before her sight returns completely."

"Months?" Sophia gasped.

Eric looked at the doctor for any other clues. Deedee and Josephine had found seats in the office and jumped from their snooze.

"Months? Why?" Deedee asked.

"These matters are rather hard to predict. The trauma left from the bullet hitting her head has caused an increase in cerebrospinal fluid. This fluid surrounds the brain and spinal cord. The resulting hemorrhaging produced the condition of increased optic nerve pressure, thus her blindness."

It seemed the air was swept from the office by the doctor's words. Eric, Sophia, Deedee and Josephine let out a sigh.

The doctor looked over his charts and spoke in even tones.

"We will keep her for about a week and administer a craniotomy," the doctor said.

"What's that?" Josephine asked.

"It's a surgery performed to relieve the intra-cranial pressure," Doctor Gluckmann said.

"Is it dangerous?" Deedee asked.

"It's not a difficult thing and she's already showing no other ill effect from the gunshot wound. The bullet may have ricocheted, causing less damage. We'll need more specialists to examine her case but we'll help her as much as we can. In the end, it will be up to Coco," Dr. Gluckmann continued.

"Spare no cost with her," Eric said solemnly.

Ms. Harvey was finally allowed to see her daughter, albeit from behind the glass wall of intensive care. She immediately fell on the floor and started crying. One of the hospital security persons tried to help her but she slapped his hand away and bounced up.

"I wanna see her!" she shouted.

"She's right there," the assistant said, pointing.

Ms. Harvey stared at the assistant and then to where she was directed. Her face was strained and she grabbed her head, rocking. Coco was hooked to a configuration of machinery. There were tubes extending from her body to the machines. Standing there watching her daughter, Ms. Harvey was devastated.

"Oh, Coco." Ms. Harvey sobbed uncontrollably, holding her head and dropping to her knees. "Why Lord?" she screamed.

CHAPTER 6

Kim and Tina sat in the detective's office staring at the decorations on the wall. They were led there and told to wait inside the chief's office amidst wolf whistles of a male dominated staff.

"They are really happy to see us, huh?" Kim asked.

"Maybe they want to have us dance at the police ball or sump'n," Tina suggested. "Mike… I mean Kowalski knows you and I…" Tina's voice trailed when she saw the smirk on Kim's face.

"Mike?" Kim asked. "You discussing my business with Mike? He's just crazy ass Kowalski to me. See, its bullshit like this I can't really go for. Why you be out there with my name to a cop, bitch? How do you sound? It sounds like you setting up Kim, right? Doesn't it sound that way, bitch? Are you snitching now?"

"Nah, Kim. It wasn't like anything he ain't already know," Tina said.

"It doesn't mean you should be telling him anything, confirming everything and all that. Think twice before opening your damn mouth once."

"Ahight already. It ain't that serious. Kim, you always trying to blow up shit. It's not that big of a deal."

"Everything's a big deal since 'em Chinese bitches bust in my place. I gotta look at the people who I hang out with," Kim said. "I know it sounds blunt, but my son could've been killed over sump'n I had no business with and that's no good."

"So whatch you saying?"

"I hang out with you, bitch, and now I'm down here because your man Nesto and Carlos done fucked-up and left everything on us. You gotta watch out and stop fucking around with bird-ass nig "

"Ah ladies," a voice said as the door opened, interrupting Kim.

"We'll talk 'bout this shit later," she whispered to Tina and they turned around, directing their attention to the person walking in with Kowalski.

"This is... ah, Tom Parker from the DA's office," Kowalski said and left the office.

"Hello ladies. Beautiful weather," Tom Parker said with a smile and walked closer to Kim and Tina.

They watched him sit down in his blue off-the-rack lawyer suit. He tapped well manicured nails on the desk before speaking.

"Did anyone tell you why you're here?" he asked.

Kim and Tina turned to each other, shook their heads and rolled their shoulders. They eyed Tom Parker, unsure of his motives.

"I didn't know shit about anything. Carlos was just staying with me occasionally. I ain't got nothing to say," Kim declared.

"I didn't know the real deal about anything until after the fact," Tina lied.

"I've got good news for both you ladies. Even though most of the jewelry has not been recovered, the district attorney is willing to stop all the investigation concerning both of your involvement in the sixty-million dollar jewelry heist. This action comes with your promise to cooperate in a current ongoing criminal investigation."

Kim and Tina held opened-mouthed stares at Tom parker. They sat up and looked at each other as if they didn't believe what they were hearing. Tina's expression of surprise was replaced by a confident smile. She had ice stashed big enough to sink a small island. She pinched Kim but Kim's look was one of caution.

"Exactly what we gotta do? I mean, I don't think I should have to do anything since I didn't know nothing," Kim said, folding her arms and sitting back.

"We know you were dating or seeing Carlos Mendez and he has been identified as an accomplice in armed robbery. You are a subject and, if not our office, perhaps the FBI will find a way to nail you as an accessory to the robbery," Tom Parker said.

"What she meant was what do we have to do?" Tina said, interrupting the stare-down between Tom Parker and Kim.

"Why is everyone playing me like I was a criminal?" Kim asked. "I didn't commit no crime. I didn't go robbing anywhere. I didn't know anything about it until them Chinese bitches shot up my place and—"

"Ms. Kimberly James, your involvement will not be difficult to prove in a court of law. You will be sent to minimum six years and as much as nine. Can you afford to leave your son for up to nine years? You can avoid pressure by cooperating with this office and accepting the offer we're giving to you at this time."

"My son? The FBI? Nine years?"

"Stop being such a hardheaded, bitch. We can at least listen to what he says we have to do," Tina said.

"Okay bitch, you've already got me into enough shit for the year and now you trying to counsel me on some shit? You best fall back with your fucking ideas, okay?"

"I hear ya," Tina said.

"Would you rather face criminal charges and prison time instead of helping the community rid itself of criminals? What am I hearing, Kim?" Tom Parker said, looking directly at Kim.

She returned his stare while adjusting her weave. Kim scowled at Tina before looking at Tom Parker.

"I don't want to be involved in your schemes but this bitch and her man got me caught up, fuck it. What do we have to do?" Kim let out a reluctant sigh of defeat.

"It's very simple. We need corroborating evidence on a certain music producer, a big time player in the industry. He's got dirty laundry. We want someone inside his bedroom, his office, his studio. His name is Eric Ascot."

"Doing what?" Kim asked and the office door opened.

"Watching," the chief of detectives answered. He walked to where Kim and Tina sat. Tom Parker stepped into the shadows as the chief continued to speak. "You may think this is fun and games but we're trying to solve a case and fast. Mr. Ascot is our person of interest. He's smart and has friends all over the city. We want to know who they are how they look and what they do when they're with him. We wanna know everything," the chief said.

"Everything?" Kim and Tina echoed.

"Every-damn-thing!"

"How're we gonna go about it?"

"Leave it up to us. We just needed your cooperation. Detective Kowalski will bring you to my office tomorrow at eleven," Tom Parker said, joining in.

"Goodbye ladies," the chief said. "Hey Kowalski. Give the ladies a ride uptown," the chief shouted and gestured at the detective.

Kim and Tina got up and straightened themselves out. Their strut gave the chief and Tom Parker a preview of twin backfields in motion.

"Well they certainly got lots of what he likes, huh Tom?" the chief chuckled, watching the backsides of Kim and Tina walking out the office.

"Yes. Ass and tits were given as his weakness in the report. They're good looking bait. Now we're ready to hook our big fish." Tom Parker added.

"We certainly will," the chief nodded. "We'll nail the bastard yet."

"Or we'll keep him spending money on high-price lawyers, Tom Parker said, his eyes riveted on the girls sashaying derrières.

CHAPTER 7

Being part of the crime scene, Eric's Range Rover was towed. He sent the chauffer, Big Charles, home in a cab. They left Ms. Harvey under heavy sedation at the hospital. Sophia gave Eric and the girls a ride to his Manhattan apartment and bid them all goodbye as they got out of the limousine. By the time they got off the elevator they were barely awake. Deedee went off to her room and Josephine initially went to the guest room but she later crept inside Eric's room.

Josephine crawled under the sheets and snuggled next to an exhausted Eric. Maneuvering her body, she wiggled her frame until she was under his armpit. Her head was resting softly on his chest when Josephine sighed and closed her eyes. She was about to fall asleep when the phone started ringing. An outgoing message greeted the caller.

"Eric, call me on Tuesday. Maybe we can go..."

"Hello, this is Josephine," she said, grabbing the phone and turning off the machine when she recognized Sophia's voice.

"Hi Josephine. Where's Eric?"

"He's asleep. Do want to leave a message?"

"Yes sure. Tell him to call me. Thanks."

"Not a problem, Sophia. I'll tell him when he wakes up. Goodbye."

"Thanks. Goodbye," Sophia said.

Josephine stood over Eric and angrily glared down at him before hanging up the phone. She ran to the kitchen and came back holding a steak knife. Josephine squeezed the handle of the knife as she fixed an angry stare at the sleeping Eric.

"If you ever cheat on me with her I'll kill your ass," she whispered.

"Huh?" Eric stirred and mumbled before snoring.

Josephine stood over him, admiring the harmlessness of his features. She stayed that way for a beat then she smiled.

"My big baby," she sighed, undoing her bra and coming out of her panties before returning to her position next to Eric. "This is my dick."

Josephine gently nudged him onto his back and began massaging his package. He was still snoring when she slipped his rising shaft into her mouth and sucked. Her fingers were lodged between her legs. After a few minutes Josephine decided Eric responded well enough and mounted him. He was snoring as Josephine easily slipped his hardness inside her moistened hole. She arched her back and flung her head from side to side while she rode.

Eric was hard and asleep as Josephine's moistness sucked him deep and deeper inside her. She wore a smile on her face as she watched him slowly stir from his sleep. His rapid winks came in surprise while she pleasured herself. Ten minutes later, she was bucking hard and throwing her head back in the throes of an orgasm.

"Oh, oh, ah… Ooh…"

Eric's eyes opened completely. He saw Josephine's naked sweaty body on top of him. He glanced down and watched as she slid up and down his pole.

"Hey. What the fuck are you doing?" Eric asked.

He knew the answer without receiving a response. Due to his exhaustion, Eric struggled to size up the situation all at once. He looked at her breasts and then her face. Her eyes were shut tight as she whimpered and her body shook. Eric instinctively held her to get her off him and stopped short when her hands held his.

"My big baby, you're up," she whispered. "I just had to get me some. I mean you were asleep and all but you looked so good."

"You're crazy and I'm tired," Eric said, pushing Josephine off him.

"What happened? I was about to come, my lover," she whispered throatily.

"First thing, I'm not your lover. And secondly what the hell are you doing in my room. I thought we spoke about this and we agreed not to do anything like this anymore."

"Yeah, I know Eric. But you got me open. You put it on me and now I can't get you off my mind. I just want you all the time, daddy. All the time, I want to feel you and—"

"And nothing. Now put your clothes on and go on back to your room," Eric said and jumped out of the bed. They both look at his hardened member as he walked to the bathroom.

Josephine remained in the room and Eric was clearly annoyed by her presence. She sat buck naked with her knees to her chest, avoiding his stare. Eric continued to look intently at her until her eyes met his.

"Oh please don't kick me out. Let me stay," Josephine pleaded.

Eric stared at her body, then her face. He felt a pang of desire welling deep inside his stomach. The sight of Sophia stuck in his mind and he took the cautionary road. Josephine saw his hesitation. She was scheming to manipulate this weakness. She shifted her body and her legs opened wide. Eric stared awkwardly at her moist cavity and licked his lips.

"You gotta go," he said, turning away from her.

His tone and action didn't convey the message. Josephine could sense Eric's uncertainty and his ever rising bul**ge** told her much more.

"I know you don't really want me to go," she said, reaching for his crotch.

"Yes I do," Eric said, avoiding her extended arm.

"What,? Are you afraid of lil' ol' me? Don't be scared. I'll take good care of you," Josephine whispered.

"No. You better go to sleep in your own room because I'm really tired," Eric said.

"I see. It's like that, huh? You only want me when you want me. My feelings don't count, huh?"

"We've already been over this. I thought you agreed we cannot go on. You're too young for me—"

"Age ain't nothing but a number," Josephine smiled demurely.

Eric stared at her as she gracefully approached him. She had long legs and a well-defined shapely torso, small tits with plum sized nipples. She could be a model. Josephine was sexy and becoming more irresistible.

"Ahight. I'll go if you insist but can you give me a kiss? Please?"

Eric's eyes were fixed on her pleasant features, her soft, taut skin and shapely ass. It was tempting. He had done it before. Thoughts of Sophia kept rumbling in his mind. Josephine moved in quickly and kissed him. She deftly slipped her tongue inside his mouth and locked her legs around his ankles. They fell on his bed and she ground her pelvis against his crotch. Eric was aroused and Josephine could feel. Her hands were all over him, his hair, nipples, and finally she held his pulsing member in her hands. She massaged his balls and rubbed the tip of his penis.

"You can't…" Eric started, but his protesting trailed down with her every move.

Josephine swooped down and devoured his hardness in her mouth, curtailing Eric's resistance. Her tongue rolled over the tip of his penis and he was harder than steel. She jerked his shaft while sucking. Eric was caught by surprise and stared at first. Then he tried pushing her away. Josephine's mouth was locked like a vice-grip to his swelling head. Her lips felt moist on him. She was sucking and playing with his balls. Eric moved around, squirming, but not offering anymore resistance. He stopped moving around and let Josephine do her thing.

"You want some?" Josephine asked rubbing her hands all over her body and licking her lips.

Eric smiled and shook his head. He wanted her but wouldn't give in. Lying on his back, he wagged his finger.

"No Josephine. I can't do this anymore," Eric said.

"Don't you love me?" she asked, rubbing her hands over her hips. Eric swallowed hard.

"I can't love you. Even though I'm not with her, I happen to love someone else," Eric said.

"I don't understand. I love you. You don't want me? Just because I'm not an attorney, I'm not good enough for you, huh?"

"Josephine, it has nothing to do with what you're saying," Eric said.

"No, no it doesn't? Then what is it huh? Whenever you feel like you just bone Josephine? That's what it is, huh, Eric? I'm nothing to you huh? Just another notch under your belt? That's all I am?"

"C'mon Josephine. You know we already had this discussion. You're a good girl but it's not cool right now."

"Yeah. What? I'm a good girl but not good enough to be your girl?"

"That's not it," Eric said.

"Then you tell me what it is, Eric. It's bullshit right?"

"No. It's just you think you're in love but you're too young to really know what love is. You're still a teenager and don't know the difference between having crushes on someone you admire. It's puppy love."

"Puppy love?"

"Yeah, puppy love. You're imagining being in love without first experiencing real love. This could happen with a person you look up to, like a father figure, or a role model. Maybe your favorite musician…" Eric's voice dropped when he saw the disappointment on Josephine's face as he explained.

"That's it. Take the little girl's cookies and fuck her over, right Eric? You're soooo full of shit, Eric! You heard me? So full of shit! Oh by the way. Your ex fiancée wants you to call her and if you suck up right, maybe you can go out together. I m sure you can use the chance to grovel at her feet, Josephine said.

"Sophia called?" Eric asked, sounding jovial and elated. The message sent a jolt of energy racing through his body. Josephine witnessed the change in his attitude.

"Ah, go fuck yourself!" Josephine scowled and strutted out the door.

Eric shook his head while his eyes were peeled on her seductive curves. He bit the sardonic grin from his lips. Eric hurried to the bathroom and turned on the cold shower. He stepped into the hail of water and closed his eyes while pondering what he could do to prevent losing Sophia.

CHAPTER 8

Deedee visited Coco at the hospital regularly. Ms. Harvey was always there. Hospital security knew the mother and often allowed her to visit during non-visitors hours.

"Is it me or are the doctors looking like kids up in here? I don't know what it is. I came to see Coco yesterday and I was staring at the doctor. I had to ask him if he was a student or just pretending to be a doctor," Ms. Harvey said and Deedee smiled.

"Coco, is she… has anything changed in her condition?" Deedee asked.

"No," Ms. Harvey said, shaking her head. "She's the same way as yesterday, just lying there on a respirator with all them wires shoved up in her and she's breathing through tubes like she's a damn robot. If only she'd listened to me, none of this would've happened. Sometimes when your head is tough, your ass takes a beating and becomes soft. Coco knows there are dangers. She never feels like she'll be the one but now she's lying there, not moving, can't see nothing..." Ms. Harvey's voice trailed as she broke down sobbing.

Deedee hugged her and helped the grieving woman get to her feet. They walked to the hospital room where Coco was lying on her back, recovering from surgery. Deedee felt a strange tremor shooting through her body as she entered the room. She watched the lights flashing on the respirator machine and her best friend's chest slowly rising up and down.

Tears streamed from both of the visitors' eyes. They sat in chairs close to the bed. The craniotomy had been successful and Coco was facing the task of a long recuperation process. Ms. Harvey touched her daughter's hand and bit her lips but couldn't hold back her flood of emotion. She dropped to her knees and cried loudly. Deedee watched her for a minute then walked over and put her hand on her shoulder.

"You were there, weren't you? Why didn't you get shot? Why it had to be Coco? Why?" the distraught mother cried.

Deedee kept her hand on Ms. Harvey's heaving shoulder. She could feel the pain surging through the woman and immediately her thoughts went to her own mother. Deedee wanted to tell her all about the rape she had endured, a vicious act committed by the same man who shot Coco. Deedee remained silent with her thoughts. She had shut it out but here in the hospital with Coco's mother, her thoughts went to the moments before she was molested.

It was a Friday night and she'd just met Coco, Daniel and

Josephine. They were in the club and everyone was having fun. It was late and she wanted to leave. At the time Deedee didn't understand the vibe coming over her but she felt woozy. She fanned her hand across her face as chills ran through her body.

While standing over the saddened mother, Deedee watched Coco, remembering the assault. Forever they would be linked by the same menace, Lil' Long. At the club, Deedee stood outside the bathroom waiting. Deedee and the inebriated Coco made their way to the club's exit.

Coco, hands in her pockets, was bopping, staring at the reflections of the faces in the mirrors on the wall. Deedee, meantime, fumbled for the keys to the Maybach. What if the car isn't there, she thought.

"Remember where you stash the whip, yo?" Coco asked as she caught up with Deedee.

"Somewhere close, I think," Deedee said.

"Okay, but where, yo?" Coco asked.

"Ah, there. This way," Deedee said, finding her bearings. She grabbed Coco's arm and pulled her to the left of the exit door. "Yep, there it is," she sighed as she spotted the car, sitting on rims, radiant in the moonlight.

"It's such a dope whip, yo," Coco said.

Deedee didn't understand and glanced at Coco, awaiting further explanation. She was preoccupied and for a moment she didn't see two figures lurking.

"What's a whip?" she asked Coco.

"Some dope shit like this, yo. That's a whip."

"Yo, honey. Why y'all moving so fast, huh?" A man's voice shouted.

"Who that?" Coco asked peering around.

A blow slammed into her face and sent her reeling.

"Ketch up quick, bitch!" the throaty voice shouted.

The fist crashed the party. Coco reeled and blanked out immediately when her head hit the pavement.

"Where the fuck you running to, bitch..? Get da fuck back here and get in da fucking whip. Me n' my man wanna test ride da shit," the man chuckled loudly.

Deedee shuddered when she felt the cold steel pressed against the back of her neck.

"I sez git da fuck in da car, bitch," he growled.

Deedee had seen this at the movies and heard of it happening to others. She never had any notion something like this would happen to her. Her knees became weak as the sudden demand hit her. Deedee's mind reeled into a frenzied world of fear.

"I said get in the muthafuckin' car, bitch," he repeated harshly, bringing the weapon to her face and pushing the nozzle against her right temple.

"Please no!" Deedee begged. "It's not my car. It's not mine. I... I—"

"Bitch shuddafuckup!"

A second man grabbed the keys to the Mercedes and

headed to the driver's side. He opened the door, got in the car and started the engine. Deedee ran, even though the guy with the gun was still close by. He quickly caught her and used his left hand to slap her face twice. Her cheeks were stinging when he brought the gun in her face.

"Please. Oh my God... No..." she pleaded as terror engulfed her entire being. Smiling, he cocked the slide, loading a round. He seemed to enjoy the fright of her reaction. The silver gun gleamed in the pre-dawn street light as Deedee screamed in fear.

"Please, please...!"

Deedee braced for the bullet slamming into her body. She wanted to do so many things but it would all end because she had taken her uncle's car without permission. Deedee shut her eyes tightly and bit her lips in anticipation.

"What're you doing, bitch? Just act normal and git in da fucking car and you won't fucking get hurt, bitch," the menacing voice chuckled.

Deedee was scared, but timidly got in the car. She tried to slither to the back but the passenger pulled her onto his lap.

"I want you close. We can fuck around while my man drives," he laughed threateningly.

Deedee did not dare turn around. She didn't want to see his face. Her heartbeat was so loud, she couldn't think of what to say. She thought she was close enough to reach for the door handle, press on it and jump. Deedee tried.

The man anticipated the move. When she reached over, he easily blocked her by twisting his torso. She stared into his laughing-face. He was mocking her. Her squirming around only served to further excite him. She tried not to stare at him but quickly saw his face. It was familiar. He had been inside the club but she was too harried to really think clearly. Where? Deedee was terrified when the car shot uncontrollably into the middle of traffic. The driver showed his unfamiliarity with the controls.

"Watch where da fuck ya going..! Turn on some fucking lights!" an angry pedestrian yelled as the car hurtled by wildly.

"Yo, what's up, kid? I thought you say you could drive this bad boy."

"Yo man, I ain't too familiar wid da shit. Gimme some more time. Why your ass brought da bitch? Put her ass out," the driver said as he searched for the headlight switch.

"I brought her to tell your dumb ass where things like the light switch is. Cutie, tell him how to turn on the lights."

Deedee was too nauseated to speak. She was unmoving and stared with wide-eyed fear at the road.

"Tell him, bitch!" the passenger commanded. Deedee managed to point a shaky finger.

"Yeah, yeah. Cool that's that shit!" The driver shouted excitedly, flicking the switch. "This shit no joke. This whip can do 'bout a hun'ed and fitty, man!" The car raced toward the highway, piercing the morning mist. Deedee couldn't believe what was happening when she felt his hands feeling all over her body. She quivered as tears rolled down her cheeks.

"Please, please, don't," she begged.

It didn't matter. His hand continued to roam. She started to resist, but felt the pressure of a gun. She allowed it to happen, out of fear for her life. The driver was preoccupied. The car was going about eighty close to ninety by now. His hand roughly groped her breast. She held in the sick feeling of disgust. "Please don't... Stop please..." He covered her mouth with the gun.

Where are the damn police? Deedee thought. It didn't do much to try and outstare him. All of a sudden she remembered the face. He was one of the guys sharing a smoke earlier with Coco. His smile covered with the gold fronts she'll never forget. Deedee felt afraid and started to scream. He slapped a hand over her mouth, and with his other hand he placed the gun's muzzle against her ear.

"Click!" He said.

Mentally, she died.

She awoke with him physically on top of her, pawing and attacking her. The passenger seat was reclined and her black spandex pants were off. Her black sweater was dangling around her neck. Lil' Long was prying open her legs with his torso.

She resisted and tried to push him off. He was strong and after a couple of minutes of struggling, he mounted her. He slobbered all over her body, bit her breast and raked her thighs. She screamed. He slapped her again and again. Blood trickled from her lips. Deedee sobbed as he viciously thrust himself into her flesh until he exploded. She scratched his face. He slapped her harder.

"Don't kill da bitch, nigga. Lemme get a piece!" the driver was shouting excitedly.

The car pulled over to the roadside. Deedee thought the nightmare ride was over. The driver snatched her from out the car and slammed her against the hood. He brutally forced himself between her legs and was inside her, assaulting her on the hood of the Mercedes.

"C'mon muthafucka bust your nut and let's get the fuck up!" Lil' Long shouted.

When he was finished, the driver slapped Deedee to the ground with a heavy backhand. Then he jumped back into the car.

"Vulcha, you nasty ass. Wiping your dick on da bitch…"

"Nigga, I didn't even use a condom." Vulcha laughed starting the car.

Lil' Long threw the rest of her clothes at her and fired twice. Both shots struck within inches of her naked body and ricocheted off the pavement. The explosion caused a fall-out of dirt to settle on Deedee's tear-soaked face. Vulcha gunned the engine and the deadly duo peeled out. Laughter and music came from the Benz. The car disappeared into the early morning mist.

Deedee was down and not moving, wishing she was dead. She sobbed loudly while pulling her clothes on. How did this all begin? she wondered. Dazed and confused, she passed out from the pain.

CHAPTER 9

Deedee woke up in a hospital bed. She glanced around and then pinched herself to see if it was real. What am I doing in the here? Thoughts raced to her conscious but baffled mind. She checked herself and was wearing Versace jeans with aqua Chloe blouse. Looking around, Deedee saw the blue Louboutin patent heels she was wearing next to the bed. She scratched her head and slowly came to the realization she was laying down in a hospital bed.

"You fainted earlier," Dr. Gluckmann said, walking in the room. "Don't try to get up just yet. I've got a few checks I'd like to run." Dr. Gluckmann stopped in front of the still confused Deedee. He checked her pulse and examined her vision. Deedee examined the doctor's face, searching for answers. He continued with a series of tests. Then he smiled warmly.

"Everything seems normal," the doctor said. "Get this prescription filled at your local pharmacy and with a little rest you'll be just fine."

"Thank you, doctor," Deedee said.

She sat up, feeling better from the news. Deedee was still dressed in her expensive jeans and buttoned down shirt. She was able to flash a smile at the doctor as he walked out the room. Eric walked in and barely avoided a collision with Dr. Gluckmann.

"I'm sorry, doctor," Eric apologized, twisting and turning his body.

"It's okay, Mr. Ascot." The doctor nodded.

Eric didn't hang around for any further exchanges. He dashed over to the bed and held his niece.

"Are you okay, Dee? What happened?"

"I was visiting Coco and, ah, passed out."

"Doctor is everything alright? I mean, can she come home?"

"Yes, she's fine. A little more rest and there's a prescription she has to be filled. And oh yes, please see the nurse before you leave. There may be some paperwork or something I may have forgotten."

The doctor walked out and left Eric alone for a minute with Deedee.

"I don't know what happened, Uncle E. Really I don't. I was visiting Coco with her mother and I was in Coco's room. I was standing and watching Coco and before I knew it, I was here in this room."

"It doesn't matter now. You probably haven't been sleeping

well, huh?"

"I haven't had a good night sleep since..." Deedee's voice trailed and her attention was drawn to the door.

Eric turned to see what had averted her attention. He smiled openly when he saw who it was.

"We've got to stop meeting all the time in hospitals. What happened? You never called me back," Eric said and walked over to greet Sophia with a hug.

"What's wrong with Dee?" Sophia asked. "Someone from the doctor's office called. They couldn't reach you and Deedee may need a ride home because she had fainted and," Sophia said, throwing her arms up.

She walked over to Deedee and assisted her out of the bed. "Well, you seem alright," Sophia said smiling and holding Deedee. They hugged and shared air-kisses.

"By the way. I called and left a message for you last week," Sophia said.

"I got the message late," Eric responded.

"Your guest must not you to get it," Sophia said, looking at Eric with suspicion. "She seems bent on saving you from my advances." Sophia smiled.

The ringing cellphone distracted all. Deedee checked hers and Sophia did also. Eric finally glanced at his persistently ringing phone and silenced the call.

"Josephine?" Deedee said.

"I'm just saying, if the cap fits," Sophia remarked sarcastically.

"I got the message, but later," Eric said as his cellpone

began ringing again. He turned it off without answering.

"I wonder why," Sophia said with a smirk.

"Does anyone know how Coco's doing? Maybe we could go visit her," Deedee suggested, sensing the anger in Sophia. The incessantly annoying ring started again. There was an impregnable pause as Eric repeated his actions, checking the caller ID and turning off the cellphone without answering it.

"I think it's a very good idea," Sophia said with an acidic smile.

They walked out of the room and down the hallway. A sulking Eric followed dejectedly. The trio reached Coco's room and saw her mother sleeping quietly in a chair next to Coco's bed. Deedee walked over and touched Coco's hand. She was surprised when she felt a grip in response. Deedee glanced down at her best friend and saw the bandages around her eyes.

"I'm glad you can feel me, Coco," Deedee said and smiled. Eric and Sophia held hands while staring at Deedee. They were not aware of Coco's subtle squeezing Deedee's hand. "I know you're gonna make it, you're such a fighter," Deedee continued. "I thought I'd lost you back there. I had no idea why he wanted us so badly, but the imbecile is gone. Yeah girl, the bastard took a big trip and won't be coming back."

Deedee paused when she felt the grip weakened and became loose all together. She was crying when Eric held her by the arm.

"Let's go baby-doll," Eric said. "You can come back and visit her again. Coco needs rest and so do you. Remember that's what the doctor told us."

"Just another minute Uncle E," Deedee said.

"Okay, you got it."

Deedee held her friend's hand again. It remained limp but she gripped tighter. Deedee then whispered a prayer.

"I'm gonna be here for you, yo," she whispered, mocking Coco's way of speaking. She kissed her hand and walked out.

"How did you get here?" Eric asked Sophia.

"In a taxi," she smiled wryly.

"I'll give you a ride," he said, gently taking her arm.

They went outside to the parked black Rolls Royce Phantom. Eric jumped in the driver's seat and the doors flew open. Sophia sat in the backseat and Deedee was up front. He drove downtown to a tiny bistro where they ate and drank heartily. It was a little after midnight when Eric dropped Sophia at her apartment.

"Don't forget to get the prescription filled for Deedee. Call me about Friday night," she said, exiting the passenger side of the car.

"Don't you worry Soph, I won't let him forget so easy," Deedee waved from the backseat.

Eric watched Sophia's sexy behind prancing by the doorman. He waved back at her and was on his way home with his heavy-eyed niece. Traffic was light and Eric was moving slightly above the speed limit along the West Side highway. A few miles on the highway, he saw the flashing lights. Eric pulled the Phantom over to side of the roadway. Instead of approaching, the police shone a bright light on the car and started on the loudspeaker.

"Keep your hands where we can see them. Driver, put both your hands out the window and the passenger will do the same!"

Eric was surprised at the orders. Still, he shook his head and complied. Deedee awoke to powerful searchlights. She glanced back and was blinded b.

"Uncle E, what's going on? Why are they stopping us?" Deedee asked, rubbing her eyes.

"Passenger, follow all commands… put your hands out the window on the right side!"

"Deedee, please do what they're asking sweetheart. These overzealous police may accidentally shoot us," Eric said.

"Why are they stopping—"

Deedee's query was shortened by the onslaught of two police officers. One was dressed in uniform and the other in plain clothes. Both had their guns drawn and were moving steadily toward them.

"Get out the car! Get out the car now with your hands up. Get your hands up!" The police ordered as Eric and Deedee slowly exited the Bentley. They were thrown against the side of car and were quickly frisked.

"What the fuck's going on? This gotta be some kind of mistake. Why are you searching her? I'm Eric Ascot. This is my niece and we ain't no criminals!" Eric shouted in protest, looking at his niece.

"Boy, you better shut the fuck up and listen. You hear me, boy?"

The officer in uniform rudely nudged them and directed

them toward the squad car. He then slapped a pair of handcuffs on Eric and Deedee.

"You can't do this!" Eric protested.

"We can't huh? You just watch and see," the officer answered.

Another officer walked over to the black and silver Phantom and began searching the vehicle's interior.

"This is illegal, man. You have no right to treat us this way!"

"Shut your trap and get in the car." The uniformed officer smashed Eric's face and pushed him in to the backseat next to Deedee.

"Illegal? Illegal huh? Sounds real good," the officer said smiling. "Really good..."

"Now you're sounding like a damn preacher. What's so good about this? You pulling me over and then harassing me. What's really fucking good?" Eric asked.

The officer laughed and Eric saw three other unmarked cars race to the scene. Eric swallowed hard and prepared for the worse. Before long there were so many police cars parked, it looked like a police convention. They jumped out, checking out Eric's car and walking around.

Half- an hour later, a tow truck arrived, hitched the Rolls Royce and towed the car away. All the police slowly got back into their squad cars. With a sneer on his mug, Eric saw Kowalski sauntering menacingly over to the car wearing a smile.

"What da fuck!" Eric started as the detective got in the car.

"You, my man, are going to jail," the detective calmly said.

"You bullshitting! On what charge?" Eric shouted.

Detective Kowalski narrowed his eyes and fired a taunting glance at Eric before speaking.

"This car has been reported stolen," he smirked. "So far it looks like possession of a stolen vehicle, resisting arrest, driving over the speed limit, and driving while intoxicated are a few charges I could come up with right now."

"What…?" Eric said with renewed surprise. "Get the fuck outta here!" Eric shouted.

"Who would think, the great music producer, Eric Ascot would be part of a car theft-ring?" Kowalski said, shaking his head.

"It's all a mistake. It's got to be. Somebody fucked up and is trying to set me up," Eric said.

"Yeah buddy, you sure did," Detective Kowalski said as he got out the car and answered. "Read them their rights then take his ass in and lock him up."

"What about the girl?'

"Lock her up too," Kowalski answered with a smirk.

Eric Ascot and Deedee were led away in handcuffs. Deedee saw a look of surprise and disgust written all over her uncle's face.

CHAPTER 10

"I told you before you need to stop smoking, 'dro. It's fucking with your weak-ass mind, bitch," Kim said, looking at Tina.

"Oh, I see 'em Calvin Klein's pills you droppin' fucking with your memory, bitch?" Tina frowned.

"Huh? I don't know what you're talking 'bout,."

"Whateva," Tina chuckled. "As I was saying before I was rudely interrupted by "

"You better watch what you about to say to me, bitch. It may not be much, but it's still my house," Kim reminded Tina.

After their meeting with the district attorney, both Kim and Tina rode back uptown to Kim's apartment. They started cleaning up some of the damage caused by the search made by the CALI6, a hit squad sent after Ernesto and partners, including Carlos. They were were killed and some of the diamonds they stole were found. But not all. Tina had stashed a sizable rock.

"As I was about to say, we can help these people out and have our way. Sell this rock and let it rain."

"Oh, yeah? Rain where? In jail, bitch? You get too mixed up in shit too quick. You can't feel no rain behind bars, bitch," Kim said, picking up pillows and setting them back in place on the sofa.

"Kim tell me the truth. You scared, huh?"

"Oh no. It's not a matter of scared. I don't know what's-his-face?"

"You mean, ah, Eric Ascot? Mister Money-man."

"Why you sound like you hating?"

"They got money and it's been a long time since I've gone shopping. I seen shit that I like too, Chinchilla fur I want…"

"Yeah, so you gonna bring down another man to get what you want, Tina?"

"Bitch, I ain't fucking with the DA for me only. It's for Angel, you and Roshawn too. Duh… the nigga is a hot producer. He got mad dough all day long. For me, every day's the same struggle. Shit cost and I gotta eat. You gotta make up your mind and be bold. Being scared will only leave you starving in this cold-ass world," Tina said.

Kimberlys thought about what Tina said and finished

putting all the pillows in place. She walked to the kitchen and poured two glasses of red Sangria. She walked back and handed a glass to Tina. They sat and drank together.

"I hear you, Tina. At least he works for his. I feel cheap doing this gig," Kim said.

"Yeah, but lemme tell ya, them checks we'll be getting, they go to child support. Every payday we can put our checks in a bank too. Get a card and only take out what we need. Some people have three jobs and don't have a payday. There's a difference between getting paid and working to get paid. One you have money, the other you don't."

They both laughed and drank some more. Tina lit a blunt before continuing.

"Hold up. Lemme steam some cinnamon sticks and burn some incense," Kim said.

"We don't want to depend on no man for our kids," Tina continued when Kim rejoined her. "We gotta go get it, girl. Get that paper and that's what this caper is all about, money and a little enjoyment. All niggas about is, 'What you cooking?' and 'Can I come over?' Sorry nigga. Stay your black-ass over your home and smell the eight course meal over the phone, playa. We won't need no man when we can do it on our own."

"Uh, huh" Kim said with a high-five.

"When shit hit the fan, we only got us," Tina said. "My girl," Tina shouted and passed the blunt. Kim puffed before she spoke.

"I wasn't planning on getting down with this biz like that but I can see your point," she said.

"I should've broken it down to you before this but it came together when we went to meet the DA people," Tina said. "Then it made sense. We help them, they help us. It's a mutual agreement. It ain't like we ratting anybody out," Tina said. There was urgency in her tone. Kimberly lowered her eyelids in deep thought.

"One day, I do wanna have my own money," Kimberly said, still not totally sounding convinced. "I won't have to borrow money. And go shake my ass all over hell to get loot."

"Nope," Tina said shaking her head. "Kim, hello, I told you ma, you'll never need anyone else to help you. Roshawn's education, ma..." Tina swiped her hand across her neck. "It's no longer a problem."

"Anyways, this reminds me of the time Deja had one of his bright ideas. I loaned him my hard-earned six-hundred dollars. Mind you, I'm the one shaking this booty," Kim said, sliding her hands over her curvaceous ass. She pointed her index finger at Tina before continuing. "You know? I was putting this fine ass out there so my son can look good. Comes time for him to pay me back, he straight-up forgets." Kim paused and looked into Tina's eyes. "When it's time, are you gonna forget, Tina?" she asked.

"I'm telling you girl, he's no different than any other man out there. You know I got you, ma," Tina said.

"I'm tired of these trifling-ass-niggas." Kim chuckled as she spoke. "I mean, my son's father, God bless his soul, is not with him, but they did things together. You know? Deja took Roshawn to the park and all. They watched basketball and cartoons together." Kimberly raised her eyes to ceiling as the words left her mouth.

"Yeah, Roshawn's father God bless his soul, was a big time basketball and video-game freak," Tina laughed. "Shit, he even got me and Angel watching and playing some shit with him. For real, for real."

"Cash rules," Kim said. They laughed as she continued. "I don't wanna stay broke."

"Yes and get any nice expensive shits you want too," Tina laughed and gave Kimberly a high-five. "We'll be ballin', girl."

"With my ass looking fine," Kimberly said, shaking her hand around before slapping Tina's bubble. "I'll be having not only niggas serving me but nice guys too," she continued. "Bitches ballin'! Yes!"

"Success bitch," Tina shouted.

"Alright bitch, be easy. My son is taking a nap. "Don't be coming to my place with your ghetto acting self, making noise, bitch!"

"My bad, bitch. Soon you'll own a house and me and Junior will come over and scream all we want."

"Think so? Don't be making all your plans for my place.

Ain't shit going down in there, I'll throw a little... No. A big party, but that's enough. Having my place run down by all these ghetto-acting ass niggas and bitches? Nigga pu-leeze, no fucking way. You know niggas don't pay for nothing when they break it. Am I wrong?"

"You right, Kim. Keep them niggas out the mansion," Tina laughed.

"If a nigga gets lucky and I do mean lucky and stay over and he better be able to buy more than Ihop. I'm talking lobsters and pearls. You smell me, Tina?"

"He better be all this and that," Tina smiled, spreading her hands wide apart.

"That's what's up." Kim said and walked away briefly to check on Roshawn.

By the time Kimberly returned, Tina's thoughts were still simmering. Kim watched as she hurriedly jotted notes on a sheet of paper.

"You look as though you can hardly wait," Kim laughed.

"You know I just lost Nesto but I'm through grieving his ass. I got a nice size rock to lean back on though. Sometimes I gotta pinch myself to know I'm still living. You heard me? The nigga endangered our lives and now's the damn payoff for all our problems. We're gonna have to flip the game and bring it," Tina said. "Make sense don't it?"

"Yes it does."

"Then let's make these dollars we know we can. All

we've gotta do is cooperate with the DA and we can be paid. They're not gonna let anything happen to us and we could sell this rock. It's worth at least a mill. Nesto done told me that."

Tina looked at her best friend Kimberly, trying to figure which way she was going. Kimberly looked away, deep in her thoughts. Tina looked at Kimberly some more and knew she had flipped her best friend's switch. Tina's round eyes floated to the television and saw the bronzed flowerpot next to the set. She noticed how the plant leaves glowed in the sunlight. Then Kimberly spoke.

"Life's a pimp and I'm his pussy girl," Kimberly said. "Let's go out hustle and bring him goodies. I have to support my son," continued Kimberly in hushed tones. "Deja, God rest his soul, can rest easier when they find his killers." There was a rustling and after a short pause, she shouted to her son. "Roshawn, is everything all right, hon? Mommy will be right there."

Kim got up and placed the empty cup in the kitchen sink. The clang of metal collided with the thoughts of Tina. She smiled at the victory.

"Alright. We're gonna be working with the great Eric Ascot."

"I don't wanna think about it just right now. You know what they say."

"What they say, bitch?"

"Don't count your chickens before they're hatched," Kim replied while fussing with Roshawn.

"They say, 'Scared bitches don't make no fucking money, bitch.'"

"Who said that?"

"Somebody with lots of sense," Tina said with a chuckle.

"I guess we just got to wait and see what happens," Kim said, holding her son close to her chest.

"Alright trooper, I'll fall back," Tina said. Then she thought about it before adding. "I will leave you with this, okay. We got a deal, right?"

"I guess," Kim said.

"I hear you, I understand. I meant what I said in a good way. Deja and Nesto God rest their souls." Tina completed the request with the kiss at the end of the sign of the cross. "Deja he was my man. He laid down his hustle and was always looking out for his family."

"I just want my son not to have to turn to the streets, like his father did. He's gone. That's the reality. My son and me, we still got to carry on. I don't want to depend on anyone."

"And it's how I'm thinking. I'm trying to get my mind to be all about Angel Jr. Nesto was into his, always looking out for himself only. You think he'd have learned sump'n when he was locked-down, reading all them damn books, right?"

"Who would've thunk it, but homey did have a long history," Kimberly said. The revelation was nothing new to either, but it jolted Tina.

"I'm gonna miss his crazy ass but I got his son everyday to remind me of him. They just alike, except Angel Jr. is gonna have a better education. I'll send him to Harvard. Imagine, my Angel in Harvard."

"I hear you," Kimberly said.

They had been friends for a long time and both knew what would happen when they started working for the DA. Tina quickly umped at the opportunity and Kimberly reluctantly joined in. The two friends smiled at each other.

"We're gonna be alright," Tina said.

"You want to get a touch-up to your do, don't you? Let me get Roshawn ready and we'll both go to the beauty parlor," Kimberly said, heading out the kitchen.

"Your hair looks good girl. It's holding well. Did they cut it?" Tina asked.

"Now who's got amnesia? Remember, it was just the other day, duh. They did the ends. I think it needs some highlights. Let me go get Roshawn ready so we can go."

"Who styled it? The Dominican chica?"

"Hmm. It looked real nice."

"It was cheap, girl."

"You won't be singing that song anymore. Let me go take care of my baby."

The house phone rang and Tina went to answer it. She returned a few minutes later to the bedroom where Kim was fussing with Roshawn's clothes.

"Who was it?" Kim asked.

"It was Tom from the DA's office. We start tomorrow," Tina said.

Kim stared at Tina for a long beat. It was clear she didn't want to believe it. She nodded and went back to fussing with her son.

"Now I really got to get my hair did," Kim said.

CHAPTER 11

Eric Ascot and Deedee sat in separate cells at a Manhattan precinct awaiting news from their attorney. Eric's protest of being arrested for a stolen car had landed him in further hot water. The detective deemed he was attacked and hit Ascot with further charges of assaulting an officer. Much to his chagrin, Eric was re-arrested for the media and cameras. Sophia was there quietly witnessing the performance of the police. Eric was escorted by a smiling Kowalski on the infamous perp-walk, a parade staged for the camera hounds.

Eric stewed in the cell and didn't sit down once during the eight hours he was detained. His lawyer, Maximo Soto, finally cleared up the legal snafu. Eric hugged his niece when they were finally reunited.

"Are you okay, Deedee? I'm sorry about all this," he said.

"It's alright Uncle E. It wasn't your fault. Mr. Soto told me it was a wrongful arrest and all charges were dropped."

"Yeah, but it doesn't make it right," Eric said.

He walked outside with his niece and Sophia in tow to face the snapping shutters of the cameras from paparazzi outside the precinct. Deedee and Sophia slipped on their shades. Eric shielded his eyes with his hand from the flashing bulbs.

"Enjoyed your stay, Mr. Ascot?" asked a media hound.

"Sure. You know the law goes out of its way to look out for me." Eric smiled when the cameras went abuzz.

"Mr. Ascot, what's your next move?" a paparazzo asked.

Cameras panned over to Eric hugging Deedee and Sophia as the trio was walking away.

"I'm going to take care of family and get back in the studio. Do what I do."

"What about this trouble brewing with the law?"

Eric paused and looked into the flashing lights of the cameras. It seemed the world was waiting for him to break down. Eric saw past the countless shutter bugs. He smiled confidently. "I'll let my lawyers handle it," Eric said then turned and walked away.

"This is another typical miscarriage of justice by an overzealous police department. Mr. Ascot will be vindicated of any charges," the lawyer started. Eric slipped quietly away. Sophia hugged Deedee as they walked toward a waiting car.

Josephine sat fuming while watching the live coverage on television. She rose from her squat on the sofa, slammed the magazine down and walked to the bathroom. Josephine studied her profile in front of the full-length mirror. “He doesn’t think I’m worth it?” she pondered aloud, rubbing her hands over hips. “I’ll show him,” she smiled and left a print of her lips on the bathroom’s mirror.

She was still angry when the next afternoon rolled around and she had neither heard from nor seen Eric. Josephine dialed his cell number but got only the outgoing message on his voicemail. Her phone received a blocked incoming call and she jumped to answer the cellphone.

“Hello,” she cooed.

“Hi Josephine, this is your mother…”

“Mother!” she shouted too loudly, unable to disguise her disappointment.

“What’s wrong? Is anything wrong, Josephine?”

“No mom,” Josephine said, gathering her wits. “How’re you doing?”

“I’m fine, Josephine. I’m sorry I missed your graduation. We were in Florida finalizing the divorce.”

“You mean the attorney and you had to go to Florida to finalize a divorce that’s taking place in North Carolina? Hmm… what a story, mother…”

"Josephine, you've got to understand. Your father and I are no longer together."

"And I guess that gives you the right to run around with any man, including the one who is helping with your divorce, huh mother?"

There was a long, pregnant pause on the line. Josephine was frustrated and her mother's explanation for missing her graduation ceremony did nothing to satisfy her. It was downright unacceptable to her and she started to cry.

"I bought you a nice gift. It's a new Honda Accord…"

Josephine heard her mother but was too distraught to concern herself with the the gift. She said nothing and her mother continued.

"It's a great car. Your favorite color, red, and it runs so smoothly. It'll be here when you arrive, honey."

"Oh, now I got it. The reason you bought the car for me is to get me to come and live with you and your adulterous lover in Florida. Mother, you can't buy me."

"What did your father get you? Did he even bother to go to your graduation? He was too busy with his bimbo to probably even call you."

"At least he called to say he couldn't make it because of his schedule."

"Oh he called, huh? I guess he's a good parent, huh?"

"Mother, dad also sent flowers and money, okay?"

"You're always on his side."

"Mother, I don't think the conversation is going anywhere so I'm going to end it before I lose my temper, okay?"

"You're just like your father, impatient and—"

Josephine hung up the phone and threw it on the bed. She waited for a few minutes and picked it up.

"Oh Eric, please answer this time," she said and dialed. Frustrated, she angrily threw the phone down again. This time it hit the floor hard and the mobile was shattered to pieces. "The only thing he wants to do is fuck me!" Josephine screamed. "I'm gonna get even with him. That bastard!"

She buried her head in a pillow and her body heaved as she cried. It wasn't much long after the phone to the apartment began ringing. Josephine stood, and picked up the phone.

"Hey, who's this?" she asked, trying to sound as normal as possible. A man's voice responded, asking for Eric. "He's probably at the Hamptons with his ex and his niece," she said in a tone laced with venom. "And I don't have any further info. Goodbye," Josephine said, dropping the telephone and cursing aloud. "I don't know who these damn studio engineers think I am? His damn secretary? Fuck that! I ain't!"

Josephine used the apartment phone to dial her father's house number. The phone rang several times before she spoke.

"Hello Dad. How're you? Mother called me earlier and told me to talk to you regarding the settlement in her divorce…"

The frown on Josephine's face tightened and her lips pouted as she listened. Then she continued.

"I don't wanna live with her and that new man of hers," Josephine shouted into the receiver. "He tries to be so bossy, trying to run everything. I don't care what the judge orders, daddy. I'd rather be dead than living with them, I swear! Bye daddy.".

By the time Josephine slammed down the phone, she was bawling. The news hit her like a sledgehammer. It was decreed by the divorce that she had to live with her mother in Florida and visit with her father during Christmas holidays. This condition was troubling to the seventeen plus teenager. Josephine wanted to stay where she was living. She wanted to be near Eric and her mother wanted to live in Florida. Even though Josephine knew it was only a short time before she was eighteen, she still felt depressed and cried herself to sleep.

CHAPTER 12

Saturday evening out in his east Hampton mansion, Eric slept with ease. He went there with Sophia and Deedee shortly after he and Deedee had been released. Eric smiled as he slept, his mind was nestled in a world of sweet dreams. Sophia was back in his life.

They were in a restaurant and she was impatiently waiting for service.

"I'm sorry, babe, but it just couldn't wait. I mean, I-... I wasn't really that late. I was there when you received your award, and I was very proud of you."

He had managed to make it to an award banquet held for Sophia but had been tardy. Angered, her beauty shone even more than ever.

"Stop trying to be my friend. I worked for it and furthermore, Mr. Lateness, I'm always on-time." Sophia lit a cigar and gagged on the smoke. Eric reacted in alarm. The waiter rushed to the table with water.

"You're not supposed to inhale the smoke. It'll choke you," Eric said, giving the coughing Sophia a glass of water. The smoke brought several waiters to the table in a rush.

"I'm sorry, Madame, but there's no smoking allowed. May I get you something to drink?" one of the waiters said.

"I'm sorry too," Sophia said. "Keep them double apology martinis coming."

She stared coldly at Eric and pulled out her make-up case and refreshed her lipstick.

"Apology martinis?" Eric looked baffled.

"I want I want it you will give it up on the table, baby. I'm smoking and need a fireman to douse my flames, Eric."

"Let's dance babe," Eric said and softly guided her out on a cloud of smoke. He smiled and embraced her sexy frame. She was beautiful in her simple black dress, which revealed more now than Eric had noticed earlier. He held her tighter.

"Hmm..." she murmured. He grabbed her hand and swept her off her feet. He was floating on the cloud provided by the pianist. Sophia held to him firmly, not caring where the ride ended.

"Your place or mine?" Eric asked minutes later. Sophia said nothing and molded herself to Eric's body. Her smile was

beautiful.

Eric kissed Sophia hard. She put up light resistance at first then gave in. His hands met the silky black barrier around her soft flesh.

"Eric, let's go to your place. We can do whatever you want." Sophia's breath was cut off by another deep kiss.

Eric massaged Sophia's thigh. The fabric felt supple in his hand, her flesh warmed to his touch. More than a little drunk from the evening's activity, they zoomed down the highway of lust. As soon as they entered Eric's apartment, his hands quickly encountered the silk panties covering her curvaceous ass.

"Slow down," Sophia uttered.

"Just trying to be right on-time," Eric responded hoarsely.

"You don't have to do anything. This loving is here forever waiting for you," Sophia said in a throaty whisper.

Eric stared lovingly at her dress, which clunging to a toned, five-foot-eight curves-in-all-the-right-places body. The black dress disappeared with a slight shrug of her shoulder. Eric kissed Sophia's earlobes while his hands moved smoothly over her ass. Sophia sighed as her body clung to Eric's thickness. Her heartbeat galloped. It made her breath come in gasps. Their bodies fell entangled on a cloud of pillows. She rolled on top. Eric sucked her nipples and rubbed her soft round breasts. She straddled his erection. He moaned when he felt her steaming, soft moistness. His hands roamed, kneading her taut hot brown body. His touch made her skin burn.

"You drive me crazy. I love you baby," she whispered, rocking back and forth.

Sophia wrapped her arms around his neck and rode him. The cheeks of her buttocks were cupped in his large strong hands. His body was in a spastic dance of ecstasy. Eric grunted while Sophia's sweaty breasts bounced up and down. He saw the way she bit her lips to prevent from screaming. She sweated as she continued lustfully riding him through her pearly gates. Through the haze of lust, he could see a figure. He got closer to satisfaction and recognized the figure. Eric groaned loudly when a shot hit him. He was sweating as he tried running but his feet wouldn't move. Eric tried dodging the fireballs coming from the many guns of Lil' Long, but his body refused to move.

"Die muthafucka die…"

Eric jumped out of the bed like it was on fire. He was breathing hard, walking around the bedroom, when he realized there was knocking. He wiped his face and coughed in an attempt to clear the fright from his throat. Eric hurried to answer the door.

"Who is it?" he asked, slowly coming to reality.

"It's Sophia."

Eric straightened himself and glanced at the diamond encrusted Rolex on his wrist. He dabbed at perspiration on his face, walked to the door and opened the door.

"Hi Sophia. I…"

"Eric, are you alright?" Sophia hastily asked.

He watched her walking, sexily wearing a pink velour shorts suit with a worried look on her face and glancing around the bedroom.

"Thanks for your concern but there's no one here but me," Eric said, smiling.

"I thought I heard voices…"

"Screaming for you? It's my heart trying to reach yours," he flirted.

Sophia tried to hide the smile bubbling at her lips. She paused and tried to hold a serious glance at Eric, but his eyes were smiling at her. Sophia's eyes danced in delight and her expression melted into a big grin.

"Nice try. I thought maybe your teenage lover was lurking somewhere inside here," she said, smiling slyly.

"My teenage what…?"

"Your teenage love. You know, Josephine. The young love of your life."

Eric hastily slipped an expression of ignorance on his face as he walked toward Sophia.

"There's no young love except the rebirth of what I'm feeling for you, honey. You're all I need," he said and slipped his hand around Sophia's waist.

"Maybe she's just overly concerned but she certainly seemed to be really worried about you."

"Maybe she just likes blowing up my phone. It's obsession, she's a fan."

"Really?"

"She's wishing for a celebrity guy to be with her. She might be someone's next perfect picture but she's not you."

"Are you doing anything to lead her on?"

"Why we even talking about that? Let's talk about us. You and I, baby, and what we want to do for the rest of our lives."

"Okay. Let's discuss this later after dinner," Sophia smiled. "I need a little time to think."

"About another hour or so?"

"Yeah sure, about eight-thirty," Sophia said and deftly evaded Eric's lips as she walked away.

CHAPTER 13

Saturday evening, Eric took Deedee and Sophia out for dinner at east Hampton's finest restaurant. The place was brimming with celebrity diners and A-listers. Eric, Deedee and Sophia were seated at a quiet table savoring the moment. They ate heartily, laughing and enjoying the atmosphere. It brought Deedee much warmth to see her uncle and his one-time fiancée happily together again. She hoped the moment would last for eternity.

"This feels like old times," Deedee said.

"Yeah. This is the best meal I've had in some time," Eric said, pausing to look at Sophia.

"My compliments to the chef. The food was really wonderful," Sophia beamed.

"I know, but it's also your presence," Eric said as he smiled at Sophia.

"Oh, please excuse me," Deedee said, standing to leave the table, but Sophia stood and left with her as well. "It seems we both got to go," Deedee smiled.

Eric watched his niece walking away arm in arm with the woman he loved. He smiled and pulled out the case holding the new ten karat diamond bracelet he had bought Sophia. Eric placed it by her glass. He sat a case down with another diamond bracelet he'd bought Deede as well. Eric smiled and ordered a bottle of champagne. The waiter brought three glasses. Eric was about to send the extra long-stemmed glass back but thought for a second and changed his mind.

"I think it's okay," he said.

Deedee and Sophia arrived just as the waiter was through pouring champagne in the glasses.

"What's the occasion?" Sophia asked.

Deedee saw the third glass and rushed to thank her uncle then she noticed the jewelry case sitting next to the glass. Both Deedee and Sophia picked up the cases and opened them. They hugged and smothered Eric with kisses when they saw what the cases contained.

"For you Dee. Graduating is an important thing. And to Soph, your gift is for a different type of graduation. We're graduating to a better future," Eric said, raising his glass.

"This is perfect," Deedee exclaimed, slipping the bracelet on her arm. "Thank you," she said, raising her glass and sipping champagne. "I love you Uncle E and thanks so much for my gift."

"Eric, you shouldn't have..." Sophia said and her voice trailed as she became emotional. "I'm trying not to cry but I can't stop myself," she said, her voice cracking. "I love you." She continued smiling through her tears.

They sipped champagne and later Eric paid the tab. The valet brought the Maybach around front and they hopped in. Eric sped off and made it back with the quickness to his lavish mansion. They sat around watching a movie. After awhile, Deedee kissed both of them on their cheeks and ran upstairs.

"Goodnight Dee," Sophia shouted after her.

Alone with Eric, she lounged next to him as he snuggled up to her. They kissed passionately for a few minutes.

"Okay, alright, lover-boy. I think it's time we do some talking," Sophia said, pushing Eric off her.

He was persistent and wasn't making it easy for Sophia to resist him. Eric's tongue went inside her mouth and they were locked passionately embracing.

"I thought we agreed to talk after dinner," Sophia started saying but Eric was hot for her and she wanted him in return. His lips cut off her breath and Sophia hugged him. He slipped his hand under her dress and was reaching for her panties. Sophia was gasping and her body trembled as sexual feelings crept through her body. But she still held back.

She was about to give in when they were rudely interrupted by an outburst of gunfire. Eric shoved Sophia to the plush carpet and crept on top, using his body to shield hers. They stayed low as the fusillade of bullets continued flying through windows, shattering glasses and leaving splinters all over the den. For a few tense minutes, the staccato sound of automatic weapons were buzzing. Round after round ricocheted off the walls. Then the place fell silent.

"Dee…" Eric shouted, running to a drawer and getting a gun. He raced up the stairs as Sophia trembled in complete shock. She held her breath until she saw Eric running back. "She's alright," he said.

"Eric, Eric you've got to report this to the police. Someone is obviously trying to kill you and—"

"Go to the police?" Eric asked. "They don't give a damn about me. They're too busy trying to frame my ass."

"Eric!" Sophia shouted in rage. "Now you're sounding more and more like a common criminal. You're like those guys on the street. I don't understand you anymore," Sophia said with a strained tone in her voice. "Here you are trying to make up with me, telling me about the future, and this is what your future is about, huh Eric? Me living like a damn gang moll with guns going off around me every few minutes? Eventually one of those bullets are going to hit a target and you won't be able to bring me back, you selfish bastard. You're playing gangster with no regards for anyone's life or safety. It doesn't work for me, Eric."

He quietly stared at her. In a single moment, Eric regretted every wrong thing he had done in his life. His mind raced to find the right things to say but nothing seemed to fit this situation. He remembered how it all began, after his niece was raped. He had gone to his good friend Busta. Eric's thoughts went back to the inauspicious evening they met at G's bar.

They had known each other since the twelfth grade at

Erasmus High School. Busta was always into hustling, everything from drugs to numbers to girls. Eric wasn't sure how Busta met Sophia. Now he knew. He was always into a lot of illegal activities.

Busta and Eric were sitting in a booth. Eric signaled for the waiter to bring more drinks. The waiter returned with two shots and a bottle of Dom. He placed them on the table and removed the empty glasses.

"What is it then, man? You don't look right. Is Sophia putting pressure on you 'bout marriage? You know when a woman gets near thirty they gotta know the man with them is willing to make 'em legal," Busta chuckled. He breathed a sigh of relief when Eric joined in.

"It's all good between me and Sophia. I love her and…"

"So when you gonna marry her? I introduced her to you, what, four years ago now?"

"My man, Busta, let me tell you. I sing your praises and wish you the best on the daily. You did me a real solid. You'll be the first to know as soon as I set a date. It's any day now."

"So if it ain't Sophie and it ain't the music biz, what da fuck you said we were gonna meet about, Eric?"

"It's my niece, Deedee."

"Tell me she ain't strung out on crack like her mom? Is it ecstasy? Lemme know sump'n…"

Tears welled in Eric's eyes. Busta looked like he was

going through deep emotional strain also.

"Deedee was raped by some dirty muthafuckas," Eric said, trying to restrain his emotion.

"Who? What da fuck are you talking about, E.?" Busta stared disbelievingly, rubbing his mouth and taking shots of liquor to his head. "When did that shit happen? You know who the fuck the low lives are? This shit gotta be dealt with and fast."

Eric picked up the slender shot-glass and sighed heavily. He raised his eyebrows and his nostrils flared in anger. There was a fire burning inside him.

"Hell yeah! No doubt about that," Eric replied.

"When did da bullshit go down?" Busta asked, much louder now.

"Over this past weekend," Eric said.

The words left his mouth dry. He raised the glass and flung the liquor to the back of his throat. His lips came together in a smacking sound.

"And she knows who did it?"

"Some guy called Deja. Well, she didn't actually say anything. What happened was she woke up screaming. I got to her room and she told me she was dreaming Deja was trying to rape her again."

"So there's your man," Busta said.

"Well, have you ever heard of him?" Eric asked.

Busta sipped and pondered, scratching his head. He ordered the waiter to bring the whole bottle.

"I know of him. He's small time," Busta said after a while. "Just another crack dealer the world can do without. He hang

around with some of the West Side peeps. That's who supply him. Let's bag the muthafucka!" he continued. "Bum ass nigga! His boys who be hanging wid him be packing and he's probably holding a nine or sump'n, too. Da muthafucka is a rapist, E. He's got to go. Let's hit..."

"I can't be involved. Sophia got me legal and I can't be doing anything to fuck that up," Eric said, easing back into his seat. "Sophia will dump me, man."

As he thought about it, Eric realized just how intuitive his statement had been. Sitting in his bullet-peppered Hampton mansion, Eric watched Sophia cringing fearfully when she looked at him. He still loved her and wanted her but it seemed to be virtually impossible to attain now. His mind harped back to the time a year and a half ago when he and Busta made the incredibly grave pact. Shortly after Deedee was raped, Eric found himself anxious for revenge. It was with that purpose in mind he met with Busta.

"Don't even concern yourself with all that worry. I know how to handle this. It's gonna cost you small change. Put up the price tag and I'll hook it up and it will never be traced to you."

Eric picked up his beer and gulped. He motioned to the waiter for more. He picked up the fresh beer and watched as Busta did the same. They sat drinking without speaking for some time.

"Six grand," Busta said.

The bottles clinked as Eric and Busta toasted the new deal. Eric sipped his beer with a renewed sense of calm. He knew the problem would be taken care of. Busta was deeply connected in the street. Both men burped and laughed, releasing the tension.

"Aaaaaaaaahh" Eric said. "This spot still gets crowded. I haven't been up in here in a while."

"Yep, it's the same. Ain't too much changed. These fine looking ladies keep me coming here, four, five, six times a week."

"You need to find you a nice wifey and settle, big man."

"Nah, I ain't that lucky."

Eric's thoughts were interrupted when Sophia walked back toward him. He looked on in wide-eyed surprise as she undid her dress.

"I told myself I wouldn't do this," she said hurriedly.

Baffled, Eric watched Sophia slipped out of her dress and turned around showing her back. He stared at her in painful surprise and flinched when she faced him.

"How did it happen?" Eric asked not looking at her.

"Is it not plain enough, Eric Ascot?" Sophia angrily asked.

"I couldn't look at it," he regretfully disclosed.

"Look at it, Eric. It says 'I will get you.' It's is a reminder from your arch-enemy, Lil' Long. He chose my body to leave this message for you, Eric," Sophia said and let her dress fall to the floor. "Because of you some asshole off the streets carved his message into my body with a blade."

Sophia pulled her dress back on and began to walk away. Eric moved to stop her but she shook his hand off her shoulder and kept on walking.

"I'm sorry…" he whispered in a faint voice.

Tears flowed down Deedee's face as she stood at the top of the stairs watching the scene. A few minutes later, Sophia was fully dressed. Eric, Deedee and Sophia went through the inside door to the garage, got in the black Phantom and quickly drove off. The siesta had taken a tragic turn. He punched the steering wheel as he quietly steered the vehicle to the Long Island Expressway, heading north to the city.

Eric drove Deedee and Sophia to her apartment. He stopped outside and waited for a minute.

"Look I'm sorry," he said, but Sophia was already out the car. "Deedee, I think it's best you stay with Sophia until I hire some more security," Eric said, sounding sadder than he planned. "Sophia will get some of your clothes."

"Goodnight Uncle Eric," Deedee said, hugging him and getting out the car.

Eric exited and walked with her to the entrance of the building. He waved to them when they were inside the building.

Deedee turned around, waving while Sophia kept walking. As soon as he got inside the car, Eric's cellphone rang. It was his attorney. He put him on the car phone.

"Eric, how're you doing?"

"Just great. Ehat's up?"

"I need a favor from you Eric. I got two girls needing a job. Their parole officer is being a hard nose and I thought maybe you can hire them to do filing or any sort of office work. And they're some beautiful girls. Nice legs and ass—"

"I need a favor from you. Why don't you shut up already, Max."

"Eric, my man, I'm sorry. I know you don't get down like that."

"Thank you. Your apology is enough."

"Eric, what about the girls?"

"I have no work for them. Tell them I don't have the time."

"C'mon man, for me."

"Alright, send them over Monday morning. Maybe the studio engineers could use some help."

"Thanks, Eric. Enjoy your weekend."

"You do the same. Thanks."

Eric gunned the Maybach and dialed Showbiz on the cellphone.

"Show, what up, man?"

"What up E.? How're you, man?"

"Chillin'. What does your schedule look like tomorrow? Can you make it to the studio? Alright cool. Bring Silky Black and Lord Finesse too if you can. I need some of those crazy beats he's been brewing. Later," Eric said and hung up.

Eric drove to a bar and parked in the lot. He went inside and drank heavily, trying to make sense of Sophia's reaction. At the end of all his drinking, he came to a grim conclusion. Sophia was right, but there was no turning back. His conscience refused to let him off the hook. He tried calling Sophia's number several times but his fingers wouldn't dial the telephone number. What was he going to say? The question haunted him and Eric finally called his apartment. Josephine picked up and she was happy to hear his voice. He told her where he was and she was ecstatic about coming to meet him.

He was surprised by her quick arrival. Josephine walked into the lounge and all eyes were on her. Tall, sexy and statuesque, she was strutting in four-inch high heel pumps. Her rock star jeans appeared painted-on and her top, a clingy, silk blouse, revealed it all. Josephine smiled seductively when she saw the inebriated Ascot waving at her.

"Hi Daddy." She greeted him with a kiss and scooted inside the booth with him. "You look like you started without me baby."

"You're looking good," Eric complimented.

"You like, huh?"

"Yeah, I like. Too bad you're not old enough. I'd buy you a drink," he smiled.

A waiter appeared and Josephine smiled at him. One look was all it took and he was ready to bring her anything from the bar.

"I'll have a Texas size champagne cocktail."

"Yes, and you sir?"

"Oh yes, bring us a bottle of Dom and two glasses," Eric said.

Josephine shamelessly eyed him, prospects of lust wild in her soft brown eyes. She spoke after the waiter walked away.

"You're feeling alright? I mean can you handle anymore drinks? Ha, ha, I've never seen you like this." Josephine's smile was sexually inviting.

"Neither have I. But every so often everybody deserves to get out of the box they've built around themselves," Eric said. He glanced around the lounge before continuing. "Most of the people in here are itching to do something different once in awhile. We're not the same, but we function the same way." The waiter arrived.

"Oh, that's so deep, Eric. That's really thoughtful. You can tell you're a great man. Great men think great things. I wanna be your sexy mama," Josephine gushed, then gulped.

"No matter what, you just gotta be real. The world needs more real people, less unreal people."

"I agree with you. You're so beautiful when you smile. You should smile more often," Josephine said, gulping more of her drink.

"Like you. You want to do breast augmentation, but do you really need it? You're making the most of what you got. You walked in here and you can just see all the guys staring at you," Eric said with a slur and Josephine winked.

"Thank you. I just wanna please you Eric."

"It was so amazing how quickly you got here," Eric said, downing another glass.

"I'll do it for you. Go anywhere, do anything, if you ask."

"See. I might need to take you up on that one day."

"I'll be there," Josephine said and touched glasses.

About three in the morning, they had finally finished the bottle. Eric decided to leave and paid the tab. Both were drunk and Eric left the car in a parking lot. They caught a cab to his apartment. She struggled with him and they staggered into the building, hugging each other. Josephine couldn't hold her liquor and threw up in the elevator. She continued vomiting inside the apartment.

"I didn't eat anything," she offered meekly when they were inside the apartment.

"You should've said sump'n earlier," Eric said sleepily. "There should be food in the refrigerator."

Eric was already half asleep before she went off to the bathroom to clean herself.

"Do you want coffee, tea or me?" Josephine said. A few minutes later, she returned to hear him snoring loudly. Eric was knocked out on the sofa. A smiling Josephine snuggled up next to him and joined him in slumber.

CHAPTER 14

He awoke with Josephine's naked body glistening in sweat on top of him. She was riding his piss-hardened dick and grunting. Eric was still groggy from the alcohol. He checked the time on his watch. It was eleven in the morn and Eric was due in the studio. Josephine was moving her hips and having a love session all by herself. Her body was shiny from the sweat. Eric wanted to move but the back of her silhouette cast doubts in his mind. He smiled, shaking his head while admiring her rotating, round ass. Eric reached forward but changed his mind about touching her.

With her back to him, Josephine was unaware he was awake. He closed his eyes when she changed position and pretended he was asleep. Grinding and pulling at her hair, Josephine moved her body faster. Eric held his eyes closed as he heard her grunting. Josephine threw her head back as her body quivered.

"Oh… oh, oh my God!" she screamed with her eyes tightly closed and rubbing her thighs.

"Breakfast?"

"Oh snap! I didn't know you were up,I mean awake, Daddy," Josephine said while seductively biting her lips. "I would've done it slow motion for you."

"No need for all that. I got to be in the studio. My arm hurts anyway," Eric said.

"Your arm is hurting, Daddy?" Josephine asked while massaging his package.

Eric tried to push her off but was offering least resistance when she introduced her lips to his member. Josephine slid her tongue over the crown and Eric eased back down. She popped his head between her moistened lips and he was ready for an encore. He grabbed the back of her hair and she went downtown.

It was after one in the afternoon and Eric arrived with Josephine at the studio. He put the black Phantom in a parking lot and headed straight for the studio.

"Aren't you gonna feed me?" Josephine asked.

"I don't have time. I have to be on the grind."

"Damn! Slap a bitch, why don't you. Because of you, I need a new phone," Josephine said, holding Eric's hand. Eric gave her a puzzled look and shook her off. Josephine held onto his arm.

"Ouch! C'mon, girl it was only a knick but it hurts like hell when you do that to it. Stop grabbing up on my arm like you own me," Eric said.

"I'm trying to put you in a sleeper hold, Daddy. I wish you could spend time with me. We could do sump'n together all day. We could go shopping and lay around like broccoli, all day," Josephine said dreamily.

"I ain't got time to waste with you like that."

"I wish I could put you in a bottle. I'd keep you on my table until I'm ready to use you again," Josephine said dreamily.

"No such luck, huh?"

"Can we get sump'n to eat at least. Please?"

Eric remained silent.

They entered the elevator and got off on the twelfth floor. Josephine lagged as Eric walked quickly to the recording studio. The team of Showbiz, Silky Black and Lord Finesse was already there with the studio engineer, Reggie. The musicians were being entertained by two young women who Eric had never seen before. The smell of weed lingered in the lounge area. He walked over and greeted the group sitting in the sofas.

"What up? Everyone's good?" Eric asked.

"Yeah, no doubt," Showbiz answered.

"What up E.?" Silky Black greeted Eric with a handshake and hug. "Good to see you, my brother."

"E., what's poppin?" Lord Finesse greeted.

"Big things, big things. Sorry I'm so late," Eric apologized.

"It's all good. We already laid down some tracks for you to listen to," Showbiz said. "Plus we got a text apologizing already."

"I didn't text you," Eric said, glancing quickly at Josephine. "I look forward to previewing those tracks," he added. He made a note to himself to talk to Josephine about sending messages from his cellphone.

"Your girls, Tina and ah…" Showbiz started but couldn't remember both names.

"Kim," Kim said.

"Yeah, Kim. They're funny as hell," Showbiz continued.

"Your girls?" Josephine asked Eric.

"My girls?" Eric said, confusion written all over his face.

"I'm Tina Torres and this is Kimberly Jones. We're the girls referred by Max Soto. We were supposed to meet with Eric Ascot here at ten this morning."

Josephine cautiously eyed Tina and Kim. Both were dressed in short skirts and blouses revealing way too much cleavage. She tried to remember where she had encountered their faces and listened carefully.

"We didn't get a text," Kim smiled.

"I'm so sorry. Why didn't you tell me this from the jump, Reggie?" Eric asked.

"I was about to tell you but you never gave me a chance," Reggie said with a shrug.

"C'mon man, you've got to be sharp instead of trying to get high. Josephine, come here a second. Please take our guests to the lounge area. Did you have lunch yet? Good. Take them both to lunch, alright?" Eric said, giving Josephine a couple hundred dollar bills.

"Sure. Get rid of Josephine, why don't you? Hang with your boys. Can I have the money for the cellphone?"

"Don't you have insurance for it?"

"It's on my mother's plan and I don't feel like fucking with her right about now. She's gotten on my last nerve," Josephine said. Eric quickly handed her another C-note.

"It's three-fifty," Josephine said with a coy smile. Eric counted then handed her the money.

"Do you want me to bring you back sump'n Daddy?" she smiled.

"No, I'm good. Actually, wait a sec," he said, walking back to where the music industry's top artists had gathered. "Anyone need anything from outside?"

"We were eating just before you came in," Showbiz said.

"Ahight then, time's a wasting. Let's get busy," Eric said, waving at Josephine. "Ringtones are the move. The future is all about learning how to capitalize on the internet. I want to produce some songs that are catchy and download friendly."

"Once you do, it's chi-ching, money in the bank," Lord Finesse agreed, giving Eric dap.

"Yeah, I hear you, I'm already down with that move," Silky Black said.

"Sales can be just as good as album sales," Eric said and paused as a buzzer went off. "Reggie, I told you before, turn the volume down, then load the disc," Eric added, shaking his head, seemingly lost in his thoughts. "My fucking intern!"

Josephine walked back over to him and pulled Eric by his arm. Eric resisted but then went off with her. When they were out of earshot, she spoke in a low voice.

"You can't hire them two. They were down with the girls who jumped me," Josephine said in a hurry.

"What do you mean?"

"Last year, them two bitches were down with a crew of other girls who jumped me."

"I don't understand," Eric said. "Do you know them?"

"I was with a cousin of theirs and…"

"I got it. You stole one of their mans and they—"

"I ain't steal nobody's man. Don't hire them," Josephine said. "They're too ghetto, Eric."

Eric grabbed Josephine by the arm and they walked to the lounge. Kim and Tina sat waiting.

"Ah, Josephine here told me that there's some kind of friction…"

"We don't have any problems with her," Tina said. "She asked me a question and I gave her an answer and she ran off to see you."

"There's no problem with us. She had problems with Tina's cousin but that was last year," Kim said.

Eric looked back and forth at the girls, then Josephine.

"See, it's all good," he said, raising his eyebrow in a sarcastic sneer.

"Okay, I'll do it but it's only for you, Eric," she said and touched his face. Then she walked away with the girls.

He quickly made his way to where the other producers and rappers sat in the listening room. Eric sighed loudly when he got back.

"I see you've been going through some shit," Lord Finesse remarked, showing Eric the morning news.

Eric glanced at the headline from the city's daily. It showed a photo of an angry Eric Ascot sitting with his niece, both handcuffed in the backseat of a squad car. *MUSIC IMPRESARIO Ascot Hit with Stolen Vehicle Rap…Shocking DUI and Reckless Driving Charges: Full story pages 6-7…*

Ascot threw the newspaper in the wastebasket. Then he retrieved it, ripped it to shreds and left it on the floor.

"The media only want to take potshots at Black people. America wants to keep us where they want us and when we show balls and rise, they send their best snipers to assassinate us. You know me I ain't sitting around waiting for them to get me,. I'm making real moves. I'm international, influential. They can't stop me."

"Hold your head, E.," Silky Black said, giving Eric a pound. "All da bullshit the law's putting you through will soon be in your rearview."

"I'm not stressing that. I just wanna put it behind me," Eric said. "They be coming at me from all angles. Feel me?"

"You know I already went through da bullshit with them trying to pin a body on me," Showbiz said.

"I'm telling you, I'm gonna fire this fucking intern and get a real engineer. Reggie is there anyway you're gonna find the right tracks, and load them for me today or should I come back tomorrow…"

"Give me a sec…"

"Load the fucking disc and stop wasting my time!" Eric bellowed.

"What happened to the Chinese wiz kid you had up in here?"

"He's Japanese. He started dating the receptionist, they

got married and broke out to Jamaica and started their own studio."

"Word? No wonder I ain't seen honey the last time I was here. She had the nasty phatty."

"Yeah as soon as she gave him some, he jumped the broom. They had a real African wedding," Eric said to Showbiz. "Get those tracks loaded today!" he shouted.

"You sounding stressed out, dogs," Showbiz noted. "Black, you gonna have to roll some o' the same shit up for E., the same thing you gave to his studio engineer. I think E. needs sump'n to take the edge off," he shouted to Silky Black.

"I brought a special sizzyrup," Lord Finesse said, raising a jug filled with purple liquid. "A few drops will do you good, man."

They all took a shot, except Silky Black. He pulled out a phat ounce and began rolling up.

"You know I don't drink," Silky Black said, twisting the bud.

"Ah nig, please stop lying. It was just the other night we were at the club and you were drinking Moe. I saw you nigga," Showbiz said.

"Ahight, that's Moe in da club. I ain't no syrup supping nigga. Y'all can keep that. That shit be too strong. Made me forget my lyrics and all that."

"Oh yeah, like the time at a certain club down in Memphis club. I know you're trying to forget that. You only had like three shots, right?" Showbiz laughed.

"Only? My tongue got tied and my whole face went numb. I couldn't remember the lyrics to my songs or where the fuck I was." Silky Black shook his head and Showbiz continued laughing. Then the others joined in.

"That was some funny-ass shit," Lord Finesse said. "You can't handle this but that's no problem," he said, pointing at the godfather size blunt Silky Black rolled.

"This is all natural," Silky Black said as he lit and puffed.

"Man, I told myself I wasn't going to do this anymore but this shit got me going nuts right now," Eric said, sipping. "Silky Black, pass me some so I can ease my mind."

"Here you go, my brother," Silky Black said.

Eric accepted the phat blunt and pulled so hard, he started to choke.

"This some good shit," he noted.

"Black always have da good shit. I don't normally do this but let me get a hit, E.," Showbiz said. "So they locked you up for driving your own whip?"

"The muthafucking police rolled on me and arrested me. Worse of all, my niece was in the car."

"Yeah, that's fucked up," Silky Black said. "I got a daughter and I'd hate for her going through all that fuckries for nada."

"You ain't heard nothing yet. After they released us, I drove out to the Hamptons to chill with her and Sophia—"

"Say word. She's back in the picture?" Showbiz asked.

"Some kind a way. You know how women are. So we chilling and fucking last night, and some fools pop off shots through the windows."

"Get da fuck outta here!" Silky Black shouted.

"No shit, man. They shot up the whole fucking place!"

Eric paused to toke. With the blunt gripped between his fingers, he nodded while looking on it. Eric inhaled and held the smoke deep inside his chest. He exhaled and felt the marijuana smoke relaxing him. But it did nothing to hide the emotional strain in Eric's voice.

"Did anyone get hit?" Showbiz asked.

"No, everybody is alright. I think they wanted to send a message. I gotta be more careful. Plus it's gonna cost about couple hundred G's to fix all that fucking shit."

"Word? They caused much damage, huh E.?"

"What? And I just finished fixing the apartment after that stupid-ass-nigga ran up in there and shot up the place."

"Damn!" Silky Black said, twisting another blunt.

"I don't know where the fuck to hide."

"It's your celebrity status. Ain't too many places to hide," Lord Finesse said.

"Fuck it. Right now all I can do is strap up and wait. The muthafucka put a price tag on my head. I'm just gonna be strapped, waiting. The problem is I'm running out of places to go."

"Shit, you should do like Saddam use to," Lord Finesse suggested.

"What?" Eric asked.

"You know da nigga be having mad problems, cuz he was a dictator, right? Even his best friends and family be trying to assassinate him. He be throwing them off by having doubles, muthafuckas who look just like him posted up everywhere he be at. You don't know who da real muthafucka is," Lord Finesse laughed.

"He's living like that?" Showbiz asked.

"Man, I'm telling you there be so many attempts on that nigga's life, he just be having other muthafuckas tasting everything he eat and his look-a-likes be making appearances all over the place. They be fucking his many wives..." Lord Finesse laughed.

"Fucking his wives? Goddamn!" Eric exclaimed, laughing.

"That's bananas," Showbiz said.

"What the beat or that shit about Saddam?" Lord Finesse asked.

"The beat is crazy."

"Yeah, it is real tight," Silky Black said.

"I like the way you slid the guitar in. You definitely bringing it right. Whose track is this?" Eric asked, nodding to the rhythm.

"That's one of Finesse's joints," Showbiz said.

"Give me some more mid-range, Reggie," Eric shouted. "Ah yes, it just needs a little bit more bass under it. Yeah, yeah, just like that. Ah yeah."

Music thundered through the heavy Altec speakers of the studio and for the next four hours the producers concentrated their collective thoughts on the task at hand. The beat drowned the laughter but not Eric's thoughts. He was contemplating the hiring of models to be used to easily pass as him. Track after track continued to bang loud in his ears. The ideas about security measures influenced by Saddam's story swirled in his head.

CHAPTER 15

It was way past six when Eric shook hands with the other producers and the studio engineers. He sat alone in a remote office at the back of the studio talking on the phone.

"Right about six-two, two-hundred and fifty pounds, brown skinned and good looking. I'll send you photos. Get me two if you can. Money is not a problem," Eric said. He hung up and dialed Sophia's number. It rang through to the outgoing message. "Please hit me back as soon as you can," he said. His cellphone was ringing and he put the landline down and answered the cellie. It was Deedee.

"Are you okay? Oh, you and Sophia are visiting Coco at the hospital... Alright hon, I'm in the studio… Love you too. Give the phone to Sophia before you hang up," Eric requested. He patiently waited for the transfer to take place. After a few nervous heartbeats, Eric heard Sophia's voice. "Listen," he began, "I know you're mad at me, but I think we should talk."

Eric waited for a response. After he got it, he hung up. Josephine walked in as soon as he closed the cellphone.

"Remember me? Your sweetheart that you've abandoned all day…" Josephine's voice trailed when she saw the sneer on Eric's face. "Okay, what's wrong? I didn't neglect you. You were the one who wanted to play Mr. Producer all day. And by the way, Tina and Kim wanted to know if they should go home or what?"

"Oh I totally forgot. But I wanted to talk to you about sending texts from my phone," Eric said, standing and hurrying out the office.

"Well I want to remind you that it's impolite to have people waiting like that all day."

Eric stared at Josephine, trying to figure her out. It wasn't hard to tell she was way too young for him and she was becoming too bossy. What he wanted to say to her would take a very long time for her young mind to comprehend. It slowly dawned on him there had to be boundaries and he had to be the one to draw the lines. Josephine pranced like she was on a fashion runway.

"See anything you like, mister?" she asked in her most infantile tone.

"Where are…?"

"They're right where you left us all day," Josephine said with attitude.

"Where, Josephine?"

"Sitting in the lounge, Eric," Josephine deadpanned.

Eric walked out the office and bumped into Tina immediately

outside the door. He held Tina to prevent her from falling.

"I'm sorry," Eric said, holding Tina so close, he felt her breath on his chest and the hyped beat of her heart.

"I was just looking for the ladies room." Tina started to say but Josephine came up behind Eric and she fumbled for another excuse. "I mean, I was trying to find Josephine. Did you get a chance to ask him?"

"Yes, he was just on his way to see you guys," Josephine said, with a wink.

"Yes, ah, please get, ah…"

"Kim?" Josephine and Tina chorused.

"Yes, Kim," Eric said. "Bring her to the office, please."

"Excuse me," Tina said and Eric watched her as she disappeared down the hallway.

"Josephine, you cannot use my phone to send messages or anything else," Eric said. "As a matter of fact, you cannot use my cellphone in no way shape or form. Do you understand?"

Much to his chagrin, Josephine was miming everything he was saying. "Exactly what I'm saying. Ain't shit I'm talking 'bout getting through to you" Eric said, sounding exasperated as he walked down the hallway. He bit his lips when he realized Tina and Kim were waiting for him. "Let's go inside the office." Eric opened the door for Tina and Kim but Josephine tried to squeeze her frame into the office. "Here. Catch a cab home," Eric said, giving her a C note.

"Oh! This is the way you show gratitude after I waited on you all night and day. I was the one there to rescue you when she left you cold. I warmed you up when you came calling. I won't be there all the time. And she will leave you cold again."

Their eyes locked in another stare down. This time, Eric's glare was ice-cold instead of understanding. Josephine realized she had pissed him off and any minute now, Eric was about to go off on her.

"Josephine, I'll talk to you later," he said.

The striking five-foot-eight, long-legged, teenage beauty held her ground. Josephine returned Eric's stare of indifference before finally wheeling and strutting down the hallway. Eric watched her curves for a few beats longer than he intended. He was almost swept away by her backfield in action. Eric quickly closed the door and walked to his desk.

"Again, my apologies to both of you. My attorney called last night but unfortunately there are only so many hours in a day. It was a scheduling issue," Eric said.

"Mr. Soto told us you were very busy and you keep different hours, so we kinda expected this type of thing. Not so much on the first day though," Tina said.

"Right," Kim said.

"My apologies ladies. So what have you done besides sitting in the lounge?"

"Josephine had us fill out these employee forms," Tina said, handing Eric two separate stacks of papers.

"Oh, she did, did she?"

Eric accepted the forms and perused them briefly. Then he looked at Tina and Kim with a friendly smile.

"Any children?" he asked casually.

"Sons, both of us," Tina answered.

"You both have children," Eric noted, placing the forms on the desk.

"Yes, but we can adjust the babysitter's hours as long as we pay her," Tina said.

"Yes, she'll do it for the money," Kim said with a smile. Tina glared at her.

"You two have known each other for a long time, huh?"

"Since we were three-years old. We went to every school together. We're mad deep into each other, you know. We really be getting it on…" Tina's voice trailed. "Wait a minute, I might be saying too much."

"I think so," Kim said.

"Alright, I do have sump'n open but there's only one problem. I can only hire one of you."

"No. We'll share the position and you can have two for one. This is how we get down," Tina said, smiling and winking at Kim.

"You can give the job to Tina. What does the job entail though?"

"It's a receptionist position. The other girl was really great but one of the engineers married her and they started some business together," Eric said. "You know what? I can split the salary and both of you can come and do duties on a part-time basis if you like."

"Isn't there anyway you can work it where we both stay?" Tina asked. She reached over and kissed Kim. "We like to do everything together," she said.

Kim stared at Tina, wondering how far her best friend

would go to get the position. It was Tina's show. Kim decided to go along as much as she could with the plan.

"Yeah, I guess it would be real cool," Kim said, smiling at Eric, then Tina.

"Alrighty, it's settled then. You'll both work here. Look, I got to get out of this place for a minute or so, maybe grab a bite to eat, so I'll see you tomorrow."

"That's it? I thought we were gonna be partying, meeting singers and rappers and all that. You mean this is all you do day-in and day-out?" Kim asked.

"Sometimes, but my day is just beginning. From here I usually go all night or until I'm spent."

"Doing what?" Kim asked.

"Usually I'm in the studio or I'm home, trying to relax, shoot pool. I used to… Well, it's not important now…"

"Josephine is your girl or daughter?" Tina said.

"I heard you had a niece. Is she Josephine?" Kim asked.

Eric paused for a beat before answering. He was still contemplating if Josephine had told Kim and Tina about him and her. Eric then got up and turned the volume up a notch on the office stereo. He had them waiting too long for his answer, Kim seized the opportunity and jumped in.

"She was saying you're really hot. Don't worry, she didn't tell us everything," she said and laughed.

"But judging from the way you're acting and the fact that you took so long to answer, she's probably right. She might just be your lil' mama." Tina joined in the laughter.

"You probably right, girl," Kim said.

"You too have time to go grab sump'n to eat?" he asked, walking to the door. "I'm getting hungry."

"Oh sure," Tina said.

"Shoot, I better start watching my figure before they have to roll me outta here in a wheelbarrow," Kim said, rubbing her derriere.

"We get gym membership or anything, Mr. Ascot?"

"I'm sure we can work it out," Eric said smiling. "Are you ready to go ladies?"

"Yes. Can you wait a while? I'd like to use the restroom first," Kim said.

"It's in the lounge. Remember, Josephine showed us earlier," Tina reminded Kim.

Eric watched both of them disappear down the hallway. He was engrossed in a salacious stare when Tina abruptly turned around.

"Are you looking at our asses? Don't lie. I can always tell when a man is staring at my ass." She chuckled at Eric's look of embarrassment and disappeared into the lounge area.

"Big C." Eric shouted to his bodyguard. "We're going to Nobu for some grub. Follow us in a cab," Eric said, walking to the lounge.

CHAPTER 16

"The last time I saw you, you just pass out right there, Deedee, flat on your back, girl. I was so surprised I didn't know what to do. First, I couldn't believe it. I just heard all this commotion behind me and when I turn I see you flat on your back. Oh my God. I started screaming for the nurse. I thought you hadn't eaten like myself. I haven't got my appetite anymore since Coco been up in this hospital," Ms. Harvey said to Deedee.

One look at the emaciated frame of Coco's mother and the teen immediately recognized the similarity to her own mother.

"It was scary." Deedee smiled uneasily.

"Did you have anything to eat? You young girls are all alike, dieting, trying to look good. You damn well should eat what you wanna. Just eat before you get anorexia and you best believe it is not a good look. Have you seen these skinny ass white bitches trying to pass themselves off as models? Models for what? Damn anorexic. Hang the clothes on wires and let them walk around like they actresses and models."

"I'm feeling better now, thanks." Deedee smiled, realizing this was Ms Harvey's way of caring.

They got off the elevator and walked down the hallway of the hospital. Sophia walked behind the pair while her fingers were busy sending text messages from her Blackberry. She agreed to accompany Deedee on a visit to see Coco. They walked into the room where the teen lie recovering.

There were fresh bandages on her face. The room was quiet and clean except the drone of the air-vents. Coco stirred when all three entered the room.

"Ma, I could tell there are other people with you," Coco said, sounding hoarse.

"Hi Coco," Deedee said, moving closer.

"I guess the other person must be Jo. I can't see but I could smell her, yo."

"It's Sophia, Coco. How're you doing?"

"I'm coming along, thank you. Damn! I'm sorry, Sophia. I thought my sense of smell was developing, yo."

"You need to be developing some manners," Ms. Harvey said. "You keep cursing and your eyesight won't be the only thing these doctors will be working on."

"It's alright, Coco. I understand."

"Understand what? She's got to stop the cursing. By the way, the doctor told you when they're sending you home yet?"

"No…" Coco's voice trailed.

"Well," Deedee said. "She just had the surgery and—"

"You don't know Coco. She'll be up in this hospital, lying down, taking her own sweet time. The doctor said it's up to her. I don't know why they told her that. Now she's gonna be laid up until she's got bedsores. And it's gonna be some expensive ass bedsores."

"She's doing alright and I understand that it takes some time for her to be healed enough to be discharged," Sophia said, temporarily putting down her Blackberry.

"You don't know how hard it is to get Coco up and out to school in the morning. I'd have to go in her room and fight the Z-monster off her. She'll sleep through the entire day and be up all night listening to music and writing rhymes."

There was a pause and Coco used the remote control to turn the music on. The Freeway track broke into the silence like the feds on a raid.

Oooh…Now cut for me mami, oh just cut for me mami…

Just Blaze…Ok que tu quiere …she says she blow la..la…la

She says she's my baby mama….

"Turn the damn music down!" Ms. Harvey shouted. Coco complied but the beat continued with Freeway O'Sparks doing their thing.

It's the Roc in your area…post up…

Freeway movin' rock in your area…

"Damn rap music. That's all Coco listen to. I don't know how she concentrate on anything with the damn banging in her ears all day. What are they saying? Get wild and a whole of style is all it takes to be in the place… I don't understand the music these kids listen to. What about Gladys Knight, Luther Vandross, Teddy Pendergrass?"

"It's a different era," Sophia said. "I find it hard to keep up with all the changes myself."

"Oh Sophia, please. Not you too," Deedee said with a chuckle.

"And sometimes I have to wonder about the messages," Sophia admitted.

"Some of the music is raunchy but it depends on what you like, yo. You have the right to change the dial," Coco said.

"Change the dial and you switch to a video with young girls damn near buck naked and shaking their asses in the camera. You can't escape it. It's everywhere. Immorality is taking over the whole damn world. I remember when people really cared about how things are going. Now it's all about making money," Ms. Harvey said.

"Are you hatin' mother?" Coco asked.

"And whenever you start putting things in its right place, the first thing they wanna call you is hater. Hater?"

"That's hatin', yo," Coco said. Deedee and Sophia laughed. Ms. Harvey was about to start speaking when Josephine suddenly walked into the room.

"Oh I see you're all here," she noted as she came in.

"Josephine? Is that you, girl?"

"Yes, Coco it's me. How're you feeling? I brought you some flowers."

"Flowers? Okay, that's cool. What kind are they? Wait, don't tell me. Don't tell me. Let me use my super sense of smell, yo."

Josephine waved the bouquet of flowers across Coco's face. The teen sniffed.

"It's, ah… Don't tell me. Ah, they're tulips, yo," she said after a few beats.

"You're right. I got different colors," Josephine said. "I got them in red and purple, white…"

"Wow, how many did you buy, yo?"

"Two dozen," Josephine said.

"Girl, you got dollars like that, yo?"

"Just a little sump'n, sump'n to show my girl some love," Josephine answered.

"She don't need no flowers. She need to get out of the bed and start moving around before the summer ends," Ms. Harvey said.

"Ah mom, stop hatin', yo."

"Hatin'? See what I mean? If you don't agree with the thing they doing, you hatin'. Look at this young girl and how she's dressed. When the men outside see you, they can't keep them minds off nothing but sexin' you," Ms Harvey said about Josephine. Deedee started to pull down her mini skirt. "And I'm talking bout you too Deedee. That's why that hooligan wanted to come after you. You have his testosterone way over the limit."

Deedee held her head down and looked away, trying to shield the embarrassment she felt. Josephine was shaking her head with a smirk on her face. Sophia's fingers were busy sending text.

"Don't hate on my sexy figure. Anything you wear is gonna fit you loose. You're a sandwich away from anorexia," Josephine shot back. For a few seconds nothing else was heard. Coco's hoarse voice broke a taxing, nail-biting silence.

"I knew Jo was coming and she'd put you in your place. You're asking for it mother."

"You think it's me they gonna rape? Never that! It's a fast girl like her who's gonna get it at the end of the day," Ms. Harvey said, looking directly at Josephine. "And I'm not talking 'bout nothing but raising them fatherless babies. You'll see this one on Maury, searchin' through the list of sperm-donors tryin' a find her damn baby daddies! And you Deedee don't sit there snickering. You quiet and shy but shit happens."

"Okay mother, ahight already. Cut it, yo. Stop insulting my visitors," Coco said .

"How many times I have to tell you, I'm not no yo-yo. Address me by my right title or don't say nothing to me."

"I see you're in rare form Ms. Harvey. It feels like back in the days when you used to chase us out your place and curse at us," Josephine said.

"And back then it was the four of you. The other child, you know, the light skinned one…"

"Danielle…"

"Yes, she was with you and where is she now? If you're not careful and carry yourselves right on these streets, you could be next," Ms. Harvey said, looking around from Josephine to Deedee then to Coco. "See, first one get killed. Then the other was raped.

Coco gets shot and could lose her eyesight. Who you think is gonna be next? Y'all gotta realize that y'all not immune to dying. When are y'all gonna realize that hanging out all hours of the night is not the move?"

The nerve-racking silence was disturbed by a knock on the private room door. The nurse walked in and checked on Coco. Then she looked at the charts, fixed the bed, then attended the bandages covering Coco's face.

"Please. I'll have to ask you to hold the noise and laughter down a notch," she said, fixing the curtains, then walking out.

"All they get paid and that's what she does, fix the drapes. Anyone can do that."

"Mother, please let's not have anymore hatin' okay?"

"Whatever, Coco. I'll just continue to pray for you and hope God give you the wisdom and strength you need to survive this cold, cruel world," Ms. Harvey said.

They stayed in the room chatting with Coco and left together after Coco had fallen asleep.

"Anyone besides me is down to get sump'n to eat?" Josephine asked.

"Sounds real good to me. I don't think I've eaten all day. I can't even remember if I had breakfast..." Ms. Harvey pondered and immediately started to ramble. "Come to think of it, since Coco's been in the hospital, I don't really feel like cooking anything."

"Yes, I'm down. Let's go and find sump'n to eat," Deedee said, grabbing Sophia's arm, which was busy on her Blackberry.

"We're not going to any Mickey D's, are we? You know

Coco love junk food. Me myself, I like to eat at fancy restaurants. I haven't been in one for such a long time. I mean any good place will do. Where's your uncle? Josephine chased him off?" Ms. Harvey asked. She had no idea of the cold chill her questions sent through the air.

"Yes, Josephine, where's Uncle E.?" Deedee asked.

"Oh, the last time I saw him he was interviewing two new girls, Tina and Kim, for the receptionist position," Josephine answered with disdain in her voice.

"This seems like a nice place," Deedee said, pointing to a Thai restaurant.

They stopped for a moment, examined the menu and disappeared inside the restaurant. Despite a bustling atmosphere and the impersonal evening crowd, they were seated quickly by an easy going maitre d .

Josephine and Deedee sat facing Ms. Harvey and Sophia. They ordered appetizers and drank water amongst the light chatter.

"Make my water with lemon, please. Thank you," Josephine requested.

Deedee tried not to stare at Ms. Harvey but couldn't help but noticing how strikingly close her mother and Coco's mother appeared to be. Maybe it was the drug abuser's persona, Deedee thought.

"You can have anything you desire," she said and smiled at the seemingly nervous Ms. Harvey. "It's on me."

"You sure? Thank you. Coco has some nice friends. Your father is the music producer, right?"

"No, he's my uncle."

"And you're getting married to him soon, right?" Ms. Harvey asked Sophia sizing up the issues.

The waiter delivered water with lemon along with appetizers to the table. Josephine was in the midst of enjoying a sip of the water with lemon when Ms. Harvey addressed her.

"And you gotta huge puppy-dog crush on him. This situation's bothering you, huh? Child you've got a lot of living to do. You've gotta life to live girl. Don't let this little thing bother you," she said to Josephine.

Josephine spewed water from her mouth. The waiter rushed back. Deedee watched Sophia's expression go to wide mouth surprise. She didn't want to look at the perceptive Ms. Harvey's face.

"Everything alright?" the waiter asked, giving Josephine extra towels.

Their meals arrived at the height of chaos and tension. Josephine continued wiping at her jeans. She barely touched the food placed in front of her. Ms. Harvey ate heartily, while Deedee and Sophia pinched their meals. Sophia was still busy on her Blackberry while Deedee was finding it difficult to hold the laughter building inside her gut.

"Excuse me," Josephine said standing up to leave the table. "We all got to live in our own private hell," she said and walked away.

Sophia and Deedee burst in an uproariously loud laughter when she was out of hearing distance. Ms. Harvey watched the two for a beat before speaking.

"Why are you laughing at her? Is there sump'n else going on?" she asked.

Deedee and Sophia continued to laugh without giving her an answer. Ms. Harvey wore a smug look as she enjoyed the meal. Later Josephine returned with tears in her eyes.

"I didn't mean to upset you. You're a nice girl and men will take advantage of nice girls," Ms. Harvey said in a soothing voice. "Look at me. Coco's father was my first lover. He put me on to sex, drugs and music. When the drugs ran out, he left me to raise Coco and my addiction. Men aren't worth it. They trifling."

Deedee held her laughter in and Sophia picked at her meal with one hand while punching the keys of her Blackberry with the other.

"It's nothing you said. You're only speaking your mind. I understand. It's just that my parents are divorced and, right now, it's been a real difficult time for me," Josephine said. "I've always lived with my parents and the whole situation is so hard to accept."

"See, now aren't you two sorry for laughing at this poor girl? Her parents got divorce and it's not easy for her. But honey, remember when the going gets tough, the tough gets going. It's never easy to adjust. I'm still making adjustments from the time Coco's father left. Some things I've done, I've regretted, and some worked out alright. I still thank God for making me live and I pray for my daughter," Ms. Harvey said. Josephine reached across the table and hugged Ms. Harvey briefly then sat and dabbed at her smudged make-up.

Deedee listened to Ms. Harvey and turned to face Josephine. She hugged the teary eyed teen.

"You've got to be strong, Jo," Sophia said, reaching to embrace Josephine.

"Everything alright?" the waiter asked.

"Yes, everything is all-good," Ms. Harvey smiled.

After the meal and hug-fest, Sophia and Deedee paid the tab. They left the restaurant and hailed a cab. Ms. Harvey was the first one home. She wanted to refresh herself and return to the hospital to spend the night.

"Josephine, you could stay at my place if you want," Sophia offered.

"Thanks but that's alright. I'll just go where I'm at. I could be alone. I need the time to think. But thank you for offering, Sophia, really," Josephine said.

"I'm going by Sophia," Deedee said. "But you can stay at my uncle's place. I'll call you tomorrow."

"What was that all about?" Sophia asked when Josephine exited the taxi and waved goodbye. "She's a victim of her parents divorce but is she being genuine with her feelings?"

"Sophia, I really don't know. All I know is she's a changed person and I wished Coco could hurry up and get better because she's the only one who knows how to control that girl," Deedee said as Josephine went inside the building and the taxi pulled off.

CHAPTER 17

They enjoyed steaks at Nobu and after a couple drinks, Eric, Kim and Tina walked out of the eatery. They waited for the valet to bring the Rolls Royce around.

"Where to ladies?" Eric asked when the Phantom's Suicide door swung open.

"Oh, I don't know. The night's still young," Tina smiled. "What d'ya think, Kim?"

Kim seemed deep in her thoughts and didn't immediately answer. They got inside the car and Tina pinched Kim.

"Hey. What's that for?" Kim asked.

"I'm waiting for your answer, bitch."

"I'm so caught up with this car, I can't even think right. It's very nice. So this the Phantom, huh?" Kim asked as the retractable hood ornament popped up. "I got to get me one. You gotta lotta cute, nice cars, don't you?"

"Yeah, I got a few toys," Eric said, smiling.

"All I wanna know is where the party at?" Tina shouted.

"There's an industry party happening. If it's alright with you guys, we can go check it out," Eric suggested.

Kim and Tina accompanied Eric to the party. All night he seemed in some kind of business discussion or money talk about a new deal. It was non-stop all day all night meetings with other producers of both film and music. Eric Ascot was the producer every artist wanted to work with. Needless to say it kept him busy.

"I guess you gotta work hard to make all that money. When does he enjoy himself?" Kim asked, sipping an apple martini.

"I ain't here to be his psychologist. I'm trying to get rich like him," Tina said with her eyes on Eric. "He's our ticket out of all our worries."

"But he's a nice guy, though," Kim said. "And he's not bad-looking. He ain't no criminal. You could tell."

"Are you falling in love or what?"

"I'm just saying…"

"C'mon. Get back to the real business at hand, bitch," Tina warned. "Don't get emotional about all that other shit. It's fuhgazy."

Kim stared coldly at her friend. She turned and sashayed toward the bar. In a crowded room filled with record executives and actors talking business, Kim searched in vain for conversations. She settled down at the bar, enjoying her martinis. Later, Eric drove them home.

"You know a lot of people with money, don't you?" Kim asked.

"I know my fare share. There are some people who I've always done business with and they introduce me to other people who wanna do business."

"It's a constant thing, huh?"

"It's about creating business opportunities so I can hire people like you. Maybe one day you could run a business for yourself."

"Why is that cab always following us?" Tina asked, looking around.

"My security wouldn't fit in this car," Eric said, checking his rearview camera.

He spotted the police cruising behind the Rolls Royce. Eric slowed at the light. The unmarked police car waited behind the cab with Big C in it. Eric was mentally prepared for their harassment. They followed the cab as Eric pushed the Phantom down to another red light. Again he slowed and checked the rearview cameras.

The stoplight changed and suddenly with flashing lights and screeching tires, the police car cut the Phantom off.

"These toy cops are so much fucking drama," Eric said.

The cab pulled over and parked. Big C got out, leaned against the side of the cab, watching from across the street. He sniffed the lingering smell of marijuana in the air and realized the oddness of the situation, cops smoking weed. The occupants were moving fast with their guns drawn. They started slipping ski masks over their heads when Big C intervened.

"Hey Eric, get outta here. Them ain't the fucking police!" He hollered, waving his arms and signaling wildly from across the street.

Big C reached for his automatic weapon. The two men looked at him, turned their guns on him and fired. Eric saw the flash of bullets and heard gunshots. Big C returned fire in their direction. Eric gunned the Phantom's engine and peeled out.

"Ohmigosh! Oh shit! The cops. They shooting," Kim screamed.

"Oh shit. That ain't no po-po," Tina shouted.

The screeching of the cab's tires came as a surprise to Big C. He was momentarily distracted by the cab driver's hurried departure without even collecting his fare. This split second reaction of Big C was all the time Eric needed to slip away. With a burst of speed the car was gone. It was also the time it took for a bullet to find its mark in the crouching Big C. He scampered for better coverage and another round caught him in the stomach.

"Keep your nose out of other peoples business!" One of the hit men shouted before racing off to their car.

"Next time, make sure da muthafucka don't get away!"

They aimed but didn't fire as they watched the smoke of the skidding tires of the Phantom. The car disappeared in the night. Eric was guiding it straight to the East Side highway and reached 110th street in no time flat. Kim was chattering nervously the whole time.

"It's alright," Eric said. "But I have to be honest with you, there are people trying to set me up and…" his voice trailed and Eric thought for a beat before continuing. "What I'm trying to say is, you don't have to take the job if you think it's gonna be—"

"No, no, we want the job. We from Harlem. What's a few gunshots? I mean we'll be safe inside," Tina said.

"Why would they just...? Oh my God... I can't be… I don't know. Everywhere I go bullets flying. Thank God we're out of danger. I hope you get home safe, Eric," Kim said when they reached her home.

"Don't worry about anything, we'll be there tomorrow," Tina said.

Both got out and went into the building. Eric peeled out and hit Central Park. He made it home with no further incident. He dialed but couldn't get Big C on the cellphone. Eric went into the apartment and the lights were on. Josephine was in a negligee, sitting and watching television. She turned it off as soon as he walked in.

"Where have you been my love?" she cooed.

She watched him walk to kitchen and returned drinking a beer. Eric sat down and she jumped on his lap. Josephine wanted to care for him by giving him a relaxing massage.

"Daddy, you okay?" Josephine asked in a baby's voice, causing Eric to wince like he was in pain. "We're the only ones here. Let me take care of your any need," she whispered. He glared at her. "Hey, I'm not the one causing you problems. All I did was to inquire about you because it's been a while since I've seen you."

Eric continued gulping his beer without saying anything. Josephine was off his lap, standing and frowning. Eric ignored her and got up from the sofa. He headed to his bedroom when

Josephine moved to block his path. Eric stood face to face with her. Her smile was alluring and Josephine was grinding her hips like a stripper. She turned around and bent over, shaking her round behind. Josephine's black thong clung delicately to her ass cheeks.

"Fuck you, Eric!" Josephine screamed as she turned around to see the back of Eric's shaking head, hurrying inside his bedroom. "Oh, you don't think I'm good enough for you, huh Eric? I hate you, I hate you!" she hissed and stomped off to the kitchen.

Josephine's salvo wasn't the only one in line to hit Eric's tightening defenses. Kowalski was meeting with Kim and Tina. He had given them orders from the DA.

"You got to get this bag in his apartment," Kowalski ordered.

"How the hell do you expect us to do that shit? Break in?"

"You figure it out," Kowalski said, throwing the duffel bag at them.

"What's in the bag?" Kim asked.

"Just get it into his apartment," Kowalski said. "And this mission is over."

"But how?" Kim asked.

"We'll find a way," Tina said. "And you do what I ask you

to do, ahight."

When Kowalski left, Kim pulled the zipper opened and peered inside the duffel. Her mouth dropped opened.

"I ain't gonna do that shit!" she screamed. "That's some foul shit. Nothing good's gonna come out of this."

"Yes, we're gonna get off the cops' list and we gonna be on get rich list," Tina smiled.

"Then you do it," Kim said, throwing the bag at Tina. She looked inside.

"I'll do it, I'll do it even if I gotta give up some ass," she said.

CHAPTER 18

The following day Eric arrived for work at the recording studio. He grabbed a morning newspaper and quickly scanned it. Eric threw the daily in the wastebasket as soon as he walked inside. He glanced around the place and walked through the lounge.

"There's something different," he said.

"Good morning, Mr. Ascot," came a chorus.

A smile creased his lips when he saw Kim and Tina. Their tight jeans and small tops did little to hide anything. The phone rang and Kim reached over to answer it. Her stomach was in full view. She could use a gym membership for real, Eric thought.

Tina bent to clean something off the floor and the crack of her behind was clearly visible above her low riding tight jeans.

"It's a modeling agency, Mr. Ascot. They're sending you

the model you requested."

"Okay, thanks," Eric said turning to walk away. "And good morning, ladies."

"Good morning, Mr. Ascot," Kim and Tina chorused, smiling.

Eric went inside the office and sat at his desk. He paused for a minute, then begun dialing. Being unsure of Big C's status, he wanted to get new security details to relieve him. Eric spoke on the phone.

"You're right. I'm going through too many bodyguards. It doesn't matter what it costs. Just do it," he said then hung up. Eric walked into the listening booth and sat down. "Reggie, load the rest of the tracks from yesterday," he shouted through an intercom device. "C'mon man, don't be taking all day like you did yesterday."

Eric spent the next couple of hours listening to the beats and trying to put rhymes together. He listened to a few raw lines from Coco. Nodding his head, Eric put together a strong hook using pieces of her rhymes.

I-I-I'm tougher than dice…tough…tougher than dice

My name is Coco and I'm tougher than dice…

He kept repeating the loop and using other verses, remixing Nas's old line in creating a totally new sound. Now for everything to be complete all I have to do is get a hold of Nas's peeps, Eric thought, listening and nodding his head to the beat. Music was his mode of escaping the day to day. It transported him to another level and soothed his mind. Eric heard the buzzing and raised his head slowly.

"What up, Reggie? Don't tell me you didn't get all that."

"It's not Reggie. This is Kim. There are some men in the lounge waiting for you, Mr. Ascot. Should I have them wait?"

"Where they from?"

"The modeling agency."

"I'll be right out."

Josephine awoke squinting, her reddened-eyes staring at the clock. She walked over to the phone and dialed Eric's cellphone. It rang through to the outgoing message.

"Good afternoon, my love. Why didn't you wake me and let me know you were leaving. Call me back. This is your sweetheart, Jo…kisses…"

She smiled and went to the bathroom, showered and pampered herself with skin moisturizer. Josephine checked out her body in the full length mirror.

"Why doesn't he want this? He can't possibly resist me. Everything is in place, except for my tiny breasts and my big nipples." Josephine rubbed her hands over her body applying lotion to her supple skin. "I've got to get these done," she said aloud while massaging her breasts.

Before getting dressed she dialed the phone again and, after putting on a red Armani dress, she dialed again. She slipped on a pair of red heels and again she redialed. She kept on doing so until she was completely dressed. Before leaving the apartment, she dialed one last time to no avail.

"Fuck you Eric!" she shouted. "Oh, I hate you! I hate you so fucking much!"

Josephine was in a rage when she got on the elevator. She hurried outside fuming.

"You're looking real good, ma," a passerby complimented.

"Fuck you! I'm not your ma!" Josephine shouted. She waved at a cab and jumped in. "St. Vincent's," she ordered. The driver gave her a lecherous stare.

"You're looking really pretty Miss," the driver said in between licking his lips.

"Just drive and stop looking back!" Josephine hissed. "Ugh! Men!"

Moments later she was strutting through the doors of the hospital. Men of all ages, race and color greeted her in every way possible. Josephine finally gave up and let them open doors for her. Even the hospital security was lending a hand and holding the elevator for her. If she had let them, she would've been carried to Coco's room. Instead she sashayed out the elevator with two men gawking at her rear end.

Josephine walked into Coco's room to the sound of Dip-Set featuring Juelz Santana banging in the private room.

Today's a new day...
Got the boo-Yeah up in the suitcase...
Go uptown to Harlem tell that I sen you...
Tell them it's August I'm gone till September...

She watched Coco for a few beats. Then Josephine

walked over to the set and turned it down. Coco rose up from the bed. She directed her head to where the sound was coming from and heard the volume drop.

"Jo, what you doing up in here fucking with my shit, yo?"

"This a place for sick people. You up in here, pumping Dip-Set, listening to gangsta music. You gonna have all the other patients sick with this."

"That's right. I sit alone in my four corner room minding my business and listening to gangsta music." Coco sang along to the rhythm of Dip Set. "Anyway, what're you doing up in here? You didn't tell me you were coming."

"Why? Is there a problem if I come and visit my best friend in the hospital?"

"No, I didn't say that, Jo. I'm just saying you haven't been here this early in the past three weeks since I've been up in this place, yo. You got issues, yo?"

There was a long pause. Josephine glanced around the room and her eyes filled with tears when she looked at Coco. The injured teen's eyes and head were wrapped in bandages but Josephine couldn't hide her true feelings from Coco. They had known each other a long time. They performed as Da Crew, a dynamic dance, rapping, singing trio with immense potential. Most of all they were always best friends who got along like sisters.

"You see through me all the time, huh Coco?"

"You're family, Josephine, and I just sense there's sump'n up yo," Coco answered.

"Remember how we always used to get on Danielle, God bless her soul, because she used to love boys and stuff?"

Josephine asked, moving closer to Coco.

"Yeah, Dani was really crazy about her guys. She kept a list and the last one was her down fall," Coco said grimly. "I remember when I first met Cory and they were drunk. Everything went down hill. I was studying at the library and she was outside drinking and smoking with him. It's been a whole year now but it seemed only like a few days ago that she was here, yo…" Coco's voice trailed as they reminisced over a friend they both lost. Coco's thoughts turned to the evening a year and a half ago.

"A-h-h-h," Coco breathed as she sat down and pulled her calculus book from her knapsack. I could study and just fall asleep here, she thought This place is mad quiet. Wish I could take it home.

After a couple of hours, her studying was over. Coco shouldered her knapsack and headed for the bus stop. On the way, she spotted Danielle and her new boyfriend.

"Hi, Coco. What're you doing around these parts?" Danielle asked, laughing. She already knew the answer but Coco played along.

"Trying to set up one of these nice apartments, yo," Coco said and smiled.

"Be careful. There're plenty private security round here. You don't want to mess around and get caught,"the boyfriend said with a laugh.

Coco stared at him wearing Danielle's lipstick all over his mouth.. He seemed alright. And he was good looking.

"Oh, Coco, this is Cory. Cory, this is Coco, my ace boon," Danielle said, sounding a little giddy.

"Hi, what's popping, Cory," Coco said, searching for her bus-pass. "I gotta bounce. Here comes my bus, yo."

"Wait-up Coco, I'll give you a ride. I mean, Cory's driving, and we just gotta go get another bottle of Alize. I'm sure—"

"Nah, that's all good, yo. You guys go ahead and do what y'all were gonna do. I'm gonna catch this bus. Nice to see ya, peace, yo."

"Danielle was soooo crazy," Josephine said, her voice colliding with Coco's trip down memory lane.

"Yes, you're soooo right about that, yo."

"But you know what?"

"What, yo?"

There was a long pause. Coco waited and hummed along to the song as Josephine tried to choose the right words.

"You might as well be straight up with me, yo."

"Yeah, you're right, Coco. I was just thinking that Danielle may have been right. She had a lot of men sweating her and she'd pick who she…" Josephine's voice trailed.

"Yeah and at the end of all it, some nigga fucked her over. Thank God he's gladly departed, yo."

"I know," Josephine said sounding sad. "I feel sometimes like I wanna join her…"

"You're going loca, like Danielle when she first started fucking with that nigga, yo."

"Yeah, you're right, Coco. I remember when she wanted nothing to do with niggas like him and then all of sudden when Cory fucked up on her, bam, she was fucking with that knucklehead. I remember…"

It was at the finals of a competition ran by Busta for unsigned artist when the girls first saw the trio approaching, Lil' Long, Vulcha and a beautiful, statuesque woman in strapless suede dress that made even Danielle breathless. Vulcha was holding her at his side like a prize. It was obvious from her body language that she didn't want to be with him, or perhaps to be there. Da Crew remained in their circle as the trio stood next to them.

"Hey, Coco, Danielle and Jo. What're y'all doing out here? Flipping, smoking that weed? Try some o' this. This da shiznit," Lil' Long said. He offered a rolled cigarette.

"Go ahead. Spark it," Danielle said.

"Oh yeah. You know Vulcha and his new thing, feel me?"

"Hi. I'm Kamilla," the beautiful woman said.

"I'm Jo."

"I'm Coco."

"Hi. Did you take classes at the Ninety-Second Street Y? No, no, your face ... Well, anyway, I'm Danielle."

"Your face seems a bit familiar. Sixteenth Street dance classes?"

"Yeah, that's it. You taught there?" Danielle asked elatedly.

"I was a student but not for long though." Kamilla's voice faded. She seemed uncomfortable.

"Here you go," Lil' Long said, passing the joint to Danielle. She puffed and passed it to Josephine, who choked and quickly passed it to Coco. Coco declined and the joint found its way to Vulcha.

"What will y'all be doing after you win?" The question hung momentarily in the air.

"Oh, that's still open," Danielle had said.

"Why don't y'all hang wid us. Let me show y'all a mackadacious time," Lil' Long said, winking at Danielle.

"Maybe," Josephine answered.

"That's peace," Lil' Long said. He pulled Danielle away from the group and spoke to her one-on-one. She returned to the girls.

"Who he think he be, trying to be on some kinda smooth talk?" Danielle asked.

"Why don't y'all chill wid me so I can show y'all a mackadacious time? Mackadacious, huh! Lil' Long can't even spell Mack," Josephine said. The girls giggled.

"Now he's pimping, yo?" Coco asked with disdain.

"Look at them wid that big, shapely woman. Who did they

jack for her?" Josephine asked.

"Let's go get ready to tear this party up, yo."

"Yeah, do what we came here for," Josephine said, sounding hyped.

The girls walked into the club. Da Crew went backstage and took their position.

"Are you okay, Coco?" Josephine asked. "You look like you zoning out on me, girl. You know that Danielle got any man she wanted."

"Rah, rah, beat the drums. Look what it got her, yo."

"You might be right," Josephine said, smiling, but her true thoughts had her frowning on the inside. Coco sensed her mood.

"Is this about Danielle or you, yo?" Coco asked.

Josephine heard Coco's voice in her head. She had drifted off and returned with a smile. Josephine walked over and sat on the edge of the bed.

"I'm just saying, men ain't shit, Coco. You know Eric and I told you we've been seeing each other and all that. Lately he's been acting like I don't even exist."

"So we finally back to that bullshit. It was like months now, that you told me you were pregnant and..."

"That's it, Coco. Wow! You said it, I'm pregnant. I am..."

"Did you take a pregnancy test yet, yo?"

"I don't have to. I could tell that's what it was. That explains why I've been having these mood swings. Even this morning I was thinking that my breasts look full and I'm not expecting my period anytime soon. Matter of fact, it's been a while since I've seen my period."

"Are you taking your meds, yo?" Coco asked sarcastically.

"It has been a while," Josephine confirmed .

"You mean a while and no meds, yo?"

"Oh, about, ah at least two weeks overdue. I'm talking about my period, Coco. You know I don't take no meds. I smoke a little weed and lately I've been drinking a little more than normal," Josephine said thoughtfully. "I better stop drinking and smoking. The fetus could be harmed."

"I'm talking 'bout you, fool. You're already harmed, yo."

"I am. I'm sure…"

"You should be in a sanitarium, yo. You're crazy, girl."

"I'm gonna be Eric's baby mother and it feels real good."

"Why are you allowed to roam the streets without your parents, yo?" Coco asked, throwing up her arms.

"My parents are divorced and I'm gonna start my own family. I'm gonna live with Eric and our baby," Josephine said dreamily.

"Okay, I swear you need brain surgery. You're sick, yo. You're too young for him anyway, yo."

"Why is everyone running that line? Dammit! Age ain't nothing but a number, you know?"

"Experience says one person can't be in love all alone.

How does that sound, yo?"

"I should give up, huh? I've been feeling that way, Coco. You're like a sister to me and I miss not having you to talk sense into my ass…I mean, I miss how you, Danielle and me used sit around and smoke weed, drink a few brews and rehearse. Remember that, Coco?"

"It's very hard to forget anything like that. It happened only a few years ago, yo."

"Visiting you in the hospital makes me think about her even more for some reason."

"It's kinda hard not to think about her."

"I remember the time before finals and we were in the parking lot."

"I remember. I'm not ever gonna forget anything about Danielle, yo…" Coco's voice drifted as they both reminisced about the last time they both shared a blunt with Danielle.

It was two years ago to the date and Danielle discovered her new boyfriend was cheating on her. This was also the last time Da Crew performed together at a talent competition.

Coco went searching for Danielle and Josephine after she couldn't find them in the parking lot across from the club as planned. She headed for the deli on the corner. Coco saw Danielle sitting on a fire hydrant, her arms around Josephine. They looked as if someone had just lost the family pet.

"What's up, yo?" Coco asked, seeing tears on both their faces.

"It's man trouble. Who's doing who?" Josephine cleared her throat and nodded toward Danielle.

"No, no, no. Don't tell me Mr. Lover man is…"

"That fucking bastard!" Danielle yelled. "I'm walking down da fucking street to find a phone to call his nasty ass and guess what? Da nigga was riding around with some other bitch. He wasn't even answering da beep."

"Well, what? That doesn't necessarily mean she's anything to him," Josephine said.

"C'mon Jo. If she didn't mean anything, why did he make a U-turn as soon as he saw us? Huh? Tell me, why?"

"No he didn't… He did, yo?" Coco asked in disbelief.

"As soon as his eyes caught mine, he was out. The car bust an illegal U and almost caused a couple of accidents. He was up to no good," Danielle said angrily.

"Y'all know my steez, yo. Fuck a nigga! I don't want one! Don't need one!"

"He's cut off. Off like, 'See ya, Cory.' I still have some more of that ounce of da chronic he gave me."

"The one that smelled like cookies and cream, yo?"

"Yeah, yeah," Danielle said. "Girls, I say we break ourselves off a piece."

Danielle handed the bag of weed to Coco and she deftly rolled the spliff. Then all three girls took turns toking. Before long, the weed had all three mellow and chillin'.

"Fuck a nigga. There be plenty more," Josephine said

puffing.

"I ain't sweatin' that shit. That's already behind me, Jo," Danielle said, inhaling and holding the smoke.

"That shit was like, pow! A knockout sis. I don't want no more. I'm chilled, yo," Coco said.

"Damn. That's the first time I hear you turn weed down, Coco," Josephine said, taking another long puff.

"Let's go check out da competition," Danielle said with determination.

"Yeah, yeah, let's start da show outside right here," Josephine said, laughing.

"You are absolutely bugging, girl. What you had for breakfast?" Danielle asked, laughing.

"Danielle was soo real with her shit, Coco. She never pretended to be anything else. Every man who ever met her wanted to do her. I should've been more like her. I'd probably be better off. I'd know how to treat men and maybe I wouldn't take them so seriously," Josephine said.

It was then that Deedee walked into the room. Josephine and Coco fell silent. Deedee smiled at Josephine and hugged Coco.

"Hi girls. What's going on?"

"Sitting with Miss Sicko, here, yo," Coco said.

"Who's laid out in a hospital bed? Exactly" Josephine

asked, smiling at Deedee.

"When are you getting these bandages taken off, Coco?" Deedee asked, touching Coco's hand.

"Oh, I don't know. The nurses and doctors, they haven't said anything. It's like they don't even know themselves, yo."

"How do you feel?"

"I'm feeling a whole lot better than I did yesterday, yo."

"My uncle sent you all these flowers,'" Deedee said and a couple of delivery boys walked in carrying four huge bouquets.. They quickly placed them all over the small room, bowed and left."

"Oh my God. It smells like a garden, yo."

"You're so right. It's like a damn botanical garden up in here now," Josephine said.

"Tell him thank yo. Oh my God! I'm acting soo new. I've never had anyone send me flowers before, yo."

"Shoot, he needs to send my ass some flowers too," Josephine quipped.

"You see my uncle all the time. Tell him yourself," Deedee said with a strained smile.

"Tada! That's what I mean Coco," Josephine quipped.

"That doesn't mean nada, yo."

"What're you talking about?" Deedee asked.

"Ah Deedee, don't listen to wacko. She's been struck by lightening and think its cupid's arrow."

"Watch what you say to me or I'll have your ass put back up in the ICU," Josephine warned.

"Oh no, you didn't. Get the doctor. This girl needs a

straight-jacket."

"You guys are not serious, right? Uncle E. can only afford one hospital bill for his artist," Deedee smiled. "And she's Coco."

"I'm not only an artist, I'm his—"

"Remember when we first met him?" Coco asked, interrupting Josephine. "He was so cool. None of us believed you were related to him at first, yo."

"I did. Why wouldn't I believe her?" Josephine said with attitude.

"We all thought she'd stolen the car from jump-street. That's why, yo."

"Then there he was, coming to pick you up from school. And when you introduced him to us? Oh man that was sump'n. I was impressed. Right Coco?"

"I was impressed too, yo."

"Yes, I remember," Deedee said. "Y'all were very surprised."

"You can say that again," Josephine said. "But don't y'all wish it was now like back then when we all you used to hang," she continued sadly.

Their minds rewound to a year and a half ago. It was the time when Eric rolled up at the school to get his niece. Everything was all good back then.

It was late in the evening and Da Crew, Coco, Danielle

and Josephine, were about to dive into their rehearsal. Deedee, along with the girls, waited outside the school's auditorium hall.

Coco reached for a cigarette, lit it and puffed. Danielle and Josephine cooled their heels on a bench. Coco handed the lit cigarette to Deedee. She inhaled smoothly and passed it back to Coco, who took a drag and passed it to Josephine. Josephine inhaled. Then it was Danielle's turn, followed by Deedee's.

The cycle continued until the cigarette was finished. They all stood when the Range Rover pulled to a stop across the street. Eric poked his head out the window and waved.

"There's my uncle," Deedee said. "Y'all wanna meet him? Maybe get a ride to somewhere?"

"We're gonna rehearse in the school auditorium. Thanks yo," Coco said.

"Thanks. That's really good-looking out," Danielle said, waving at Eric Ascot.

"Yeah, thanks. You're always looking out," Josephine said, giving Coco a challenging look. Coco shook her head. Eric Ascot spun the vehicle around in front of the girls.

"Hello, young ladies," he said, greeting the girls from the driver's seat.

"Uncle E., I'd like you to meet Coco, Danielle and Josephine. They have a group called Coco and Da Crew."

"Not anymore. We just Da Crew, yo," Coco said.

"Yep, Eric," Danielle said, stepping forward. "It's Coco, the crowd motivator, yo, Ms. Flamboyant Jo, and myself, D to the A to N to I…"

"The love-lay Dani," Josephine said, rhythmically

completing the melody. The girls laughed. Deedee opened the door and got in the luxury SUV.

"Come check us out this weekend. We're gonna wreck shit at Busta's Open-Mike contest, yo," Coco said.

"I will, I will. Nice to have met you girls and good luck," Eric said.

"I'll see y'all in school tomorrow. Enjoy your rehearsal." Deedee smiled as the Range Rover pulled away. She waved. The girls raised their hands.

"Peace," Coco, Danielle and Josephine hollered, raising their arms in unison.

CHAPTER 19

Eric sat reviewing head shots and examining the facial expressions of three different male models. He wanted the one who looked the closest possible to him. There was one who stood out. From different angles, he could easily pass for Eric Ascot.

In order to test the subject chosen, Eric made a phone call sending both Kim and Tina out to lunch. When Eric was sure there was no one but the models and him in the office, he walked out. With a promise to use them in the future, Eric dismissed the other two models. He kept the other model, a dead-ringer look-a-like to Eric.

"Now you're gonna have to put a little weight on and you'll be good," Eric said, looking the man up and down. "This is gonna be interesting," Eric said setting back in the huge office chair. "Now I want you to listen up. There some clothes in the closet. I want you to wear them and you're gonna run this studio for the rest of the day. I got to go take care of some business in Long Island."

"What am I gonna do?'

"Go with the flow. Play me for a half a day. Do whatever you want. Listen to music, smoke a cigar and stay in the office. My studio assistant is Reggie. He's an intern. Just yell at him for anything and he'll be licking your ass to do everything for you, alright?"

"Yes, I'm clear."

"And one more thing, don't take any calls from Josephine."

Eric slipped on his Marc Jacobs dark wrap-around. The fashionable sunshades shielded his face while he raced out the office and into the parking lot. He jumped into his parked red Murceilargo, pumped it and the tires screeched loudly. Eric peeled out, racing off to the Hamptons with a devious smile.

Back in the studio, the bevy of calls was being handled by his double and two receptionists. This Saddam thing was a very good idea, he chuckled thinking. Eric called Sophia and then sent her a text message, offering to pay for her plastic surgery. He felt his stomach tightening as his mind churned. Hitting the Long Island Expressway, Eric tried to put his thoughts behind him.

He called Deedee from his cellphone. It rang through to her voicemail. Eric left a message telling her he was on his way to the Hamptons where he would be meeting with contractors to repair the damages to the house.

Deedee and Josephine were still visiting with Coco at the Hospital. The girls sat around listening to music and Josephine helped Coco out of the bed. They danced around and rapped along to Kanye West's "*Jesus Walks.*"

Yo. We at war

We at war with terrorism, racism and most of all we're at war with ourselves (Jesus Walks)

God show me the way because the devil is trying to break me down

(Jesus Walks with me), with me, with me, with me…

The vibe of Coco's two visitors had her in better spirits. After a few turns, Coco sat back on the bed, listening and laughing with her friends to music. She was unable to see but had survived. She could've been deep-sixed like Danielle. Her thoughts sparked an idea. She wanted to write a song but felt trapped by a mind full of gloom.

Despite the chatter of the visitors, Coco was still lost and alone in her world of darkness. She gripped the sheets and steadied herself to keep from shaking. No lights to illuminate her dark path, Coco braved the walk down an unfamiliar area in her life. Her fears hit her like a ton of bricks and in one uncomfortable rush, an eerie sequence of people dying came to the surface.

Danielle's image came to the forefront of her mind. Then there was Bebop, a friend killed a couple years ago. Next the face of Deja popped up. Then it was Miss Katie's face with her gentle smile. The appearance of Danielle rocked her mind again. Coco vividly remembered seeing snapshots of Danielle's corpse.

Coco could still see the cop in the precinct. She and Josephine stood at a desk nervously watching a sergeant fidgeting with the papers in front of him.

"Have a seat," he said.

Coco and Josephine sat close together, staring at the clutter on the battered desk. Both the teens anxiously waited on the slow-moving man.

"I could smoke, yo?" Coco asked. She placed a cigarette in her mouth, looking at no one particularly.

"Sure you can. I'm Officer Carter. Did anyone tell you why you were being brought here?"

"Yeah, they told us we needed to answer more questions," Josephine said.

"We already told 'em everything," Coco said, a stream of smoke coming from her mouth.

Carter pulled an envelope from his breast pocket. He spread the contents on the table; black and white photographs.

"You told the officers that your friend was missing," Carter said.

Coco and Josephine looked down at the pictures. They immediately saw photos of a girl, naked and grotesquely dead.

"I feel faint," Josephine said.

"Get her some water. Are you okay?" Carter asked Coco.

She was scrambling through the pictures. Josephine rose and drank readily from the paper cup.

"Let me help you," Carter said. He turned the pictures so the girls could easily see them. "Do you know this person?"

Josephine examined a photo closely. She saw that half of Danielle's face was gone. Her tattoo was visible. Josephine started to sit down, but missed the chair. She fell to the floor.

"Oh my God! Oh, my God! It's not—it couldn't be," she screamed, then passed out. Carter knelt, cradling her head in his arms. He held a white tab of smelling salt to her nose and squeezed it.

Coco selected a photograph and scrutinized it. The tattoo was Danielle's. All three had had hearts tattooed on their breasts, as tokens of friendship. Coco clutched her throat and lay the picture down. She shut her eyes and felt swirling as her mind spun, rewinding memories of Danielle. She grabbed the table to balance herself.

"Here, drink this," an officer said.

He handed Coco a paper cup. She gulped the fluid. He handed a second cup to Carter, tending to Josephine. Coco sighed loudly and lit another cigarette.

"I guess you guys know the person in the photo. She's been Jane Doe to us. Who is she to you?" Carter asked.

"She's our friend," Coco said.

"Her name's Danielle Richards. She's..." Josephine

sobbed uncontrollably. She could not continue. She grabbed her face and screamed.

Deedee was watching Coco slowly reclining on the hospital's bed with a look of pain on her face. She left from where she was arranging flowers and walked over to the bed.

"Are you alright, Coco?" she asked. "Are you okay?"

"Yeah. I've been thinking about death a lot lately, yo," Coco whispered. "I don't know, yo.,. but I'm beginning to feel real dizzy."

"You should get some rest, Coco. Maybe with all the excitement… Should I get the nurse?"

"No, no, I think I'm good, yo. Let me just lay here and chill for a minute."

"Whatcha need is some good weed. That'll clear up all your congestion right now," Josephine said, walking to the bed with a smile.

"Jo, you're a nut. You know that, yo?" Coco laughed, then fell silent.

Josephine and Deedee watched her for a couple beats. Both could hear their own breath as they nervously glanced at each other.

"I'm gonna get the nurse," Deedee said in an anxiety-filled murmur.

Josephine watched Deedee dashing out the room. She

shrugged her shoulder and flopped on the bed next to Coco.

"Deedee is so much drama," Coco said.

"Just hurry up and get well," Josephine whispered. "I know you don't like all the fussing about you. I can't wait for the day when we'll be able to chill and smoke some 'dro, me and you alone."

A few seconds later, a nurse walked into the room with Deedee. The nurse busied herself attending to Coco, checking her pulse, temperature and examining the bandage covering her eyes.

"The doctor will have to look at her. I'll ring for him but when he comes, both of you will have to wait in the waiting area. And please, not so much noise," the nurse instructed and walked out.

Deedee and Josephine sat in silence with Coco until the doctor came. The nurse shooed them out and they left immediately.

"Bye Coco," Deedee said.

"See ya later, champ," Josephine smiled. "We'll be outside waiting."

"Quietly," the nurse reminded them.

Deedee and Josephine exited and sat together in the waiting room. They tried to evoke small talk but it went dead after a few exchanges. Then Josephine dropped a bomb.

"Hey, I guess I better tell you before you hear from anyone else. I think I'm pregnant and it's Eric's," she said.

Deedee shot her an icy stare without saying anything. Josephine returned the favor. They both huffed, got up and walked away from each other.

CHAPTER 20

The next couple of weeks saw Josephine and Deedee visiting Coco on the regular. They often bumped into her mother, who was always in the hospital for her daughter. Coco's recuperation was going according to schedule. All post-surgery procedures were monitored by the best ophthalmologist in the business. Eric Ascot didn't spare any cost and demanded the best in the medical field.

Six weeks after surgery, the doctors authorized the removal of Coco's bandages. She was elated at the possibility of testing her vision. Coco wanted to be out of the hospital and getting back into her music. With the chance to enjoy the rest of summer, she anxiously awaited the day.

Deedee knew Josephine's schedule at the studio. She started spending more time at Sophia's and made visits to the hospital to see Coco whenever Josephine couldn't. The maneuvering to avoid Josephine was made simpler because Josephine's mother was in the city. She and her mother stayed at the W Hotel together. After Eric hired Kim and Tina, Josephine felt out of place at the office and visited Coco a lot. They passed the time chatting.

"You'll only be there for summer. Aren't you going to college in the fall, yo?"

"It doesn't matter. I'm not gonna go back with her and her boyfriend," Josephine said on a visit. "They're married but I don't think he could be my father."

"He's your stepfather, wacko."

"He's a pervert, looking at me, licking his lips like he wanna have sex with me."

"That's who your mother married, yo. You better take that up with her. Like yo, I don't how I'm gonna say this but your man be sizing me up."

"She'll probably blame me," Josephine said thoughtfully. "She told me that I'm rebelling and that my bad behavior and temper is a result of the anger I felt about how my father abandoned me."

"What you feel, yo?"

"It might be that but it's also her acting spoilt and attaching herself to the first dick that came along. She was just too happy to kick dad out and hook up with Mr. Pervert."

"I don't know… I mean I feel you should tell her straight up what the fuck is up with that, yo."

"I'm telling you, it's fucked up when your parents get

divorced. They don't care what they put the kids through," Josephine said and her voice drifted.

Coco could hear the sadness in her friend's voice. Josephine had been sheltered by her parents. Their break-up was tearing her apart. She was on her own much the same way Coco felt alone. Deep down inside, neither could stop the gnawing emptiness they each felt but there was comfort in their companionship. Josephine held Coco's hand.

The evening wore on and Josephine began stirring. She was moving from here to there in the small room. Despite fingering the remote, Coco could sense her nervous shifting and commented.

"You always act this way when you think Deedee is coming, yo," Coco said as *So Ghetto,* a Jay Z classic, began ringing out.

I'm so gangsta prissy chick don't wanna fuck wih me

Iceberg Slim ride rims

I'm so gutter ghetto girls fall in love with me…

"I think she doesn't like me too much. You better turn that shit down," Josephine warned. "Remember the last time?"

"Whateva! Later for them. It ain't even that loud, yo."

"You're soo ghetto…"

"You're the one to talk, yo. First Deedee lets you stay at her uncle's apartment, then you steal him. And you walking around talking 'bout you prego for the nigga and talking 'bout, 'That bitch don't like me. Who's ghetto?"

"Coco c'mon, you know me. I'm a loveable type person. And she goes out of her way purposely to be mean and bitchy to me."

"I think it's your paranoia, yo."

"Oh you think so, huh?"

"I mean why—"

"Coco, we'll see. Well I'll see and you'll hear," Josephine said, looking at the bandages over Coco's eyes. "Still don't know when they're gonna take those damn things off your eyes? I mean ain't it time you be out?"

"I'm gonna leave as soon as they say so, yo. Furthermore, I can see far better with the bandages over my eyes. I get to see people with my third eye. I can easily feel out fake ones, yo."

"Whateva, Coco. Check out your fake-ass friend, when she gets here." Coco ignored her and listened to the music.

I'm so gutter ghetto girls fall in love with me

You know him well… Goes by the name of Jigga

I'm so gangsta prissy chicks don't wanna fuck with me…

As the rhymes from Jay Z flowed gently in the background, Deedee walked into the room. She was relaxed in her black Armani jeans and beige blouse and beige Manolo heels to match. Deedee bought a box of chocolate from Balducci's for Coco.

"Are you allowed chocolate?" Josephine asked when she saw Coco take a couple straight down. She joined Coco and Deedee on the bed, eating chocolate. "This is real good."

"Isn't it? But don't be eating up all my munchies. I gotta have some for later, yo."

"Let me find out. You be up in here steaming weed or sump'n, huh? Why you be getting munchies, Coco?" Josephine asked.

"Get off my block, yo. Since your nosey ass is already at my front door, it's because I can't get up and walk down to the vending machine."

"Whateva. Don't give me your stink attitude, blind-girl," Josephine laughed.

"Yeah, go ahead, I told you, yo. It only forces me to use my third-eye."

"Hmm… hmm, we'll see."

"Y'all two are constantly on each other like sisters," Deedee opined after quietly listening to Josephine and Coco.

"I gotta put up with her until she gets out of this place," Josephine said with a chuckle. "Then after that, I'm gonna whup that ass."

"You can't be, serious, yo. Whup whose ass? You better watch what you say to me, yo."

"Oh, this is what I get for visiting a friend, bitch?"

"Ahight, you just been visiting me, Deedee's been here damn near every day since I've been in here. So don't even act like you been getting it in big time, yo. You still coming up short."

"I ain't had no time for your blind ass. I was busy covering at the studio. The receptionist got married, you know?"

"Oh really? That's what it was, yo? I thought it was sump'n else."

"Like…?"

"Like a certain producer…"

"Are you talking about Uncle E.?"

"He's at the studio with—"

"Nope, he's in the Hamptons."

"I told me he was going to the studio, that's all," Josephine , sounding impatient.

"He's been in the Hamptons for a couple days now," Deedee assured.

"You sure? I'm with Eric all the time. I mean the new receptionists, they told me he was in the listening booth and I know he's been working with Showbiz and Silky Black making some new tracks for the movie soundtrack," Josephine snarled. Her claws were about to extend. There was an icy chill.

"I know he's in the Hamptons. I know nothing about any new receptionists," Deedee said.

"See, that's what I mean. You don't know everything that he's doing. He hired Kim and Tina last week. I saw them when-"

"Wait up, yo. Hold up. He hired who?"

"Kim and Tina," Josephine repeated.

"Kim and Tina from 'round my way?"

"I don't know. They filled out the applications and gave them directly to Eric. They knew that girl, Pricilla, and that bullshit with Geo—"

"Them the two bitches I can't stand the most, yo."

"I didn't know it was that serious. They were acting like everything was cool. If I'd known, I'd have told Eric not to hire they fake asses. I wanted to do the receptionist gig and I was doing a good job until them two came in the picture," Josephine said.

"One is Puerto Rican and real pretty and the other is ahight, a black chick, right?"

"Yeah, that's them—"

"Jo, you better tell Eric to fire their asses right now, yo!"

"Are those the same ones who fired the gun—" Deedee started to ask but Coco didn't let her finish.

"Yes Dee, they the same ones, yo."

"Oh Uncle E. should have never hired them. I'll have to let him know," Deedee said.

"Right away, right away, yo."

The nurse walked into the room and immediately turned the music down. She fussed with the curtains and then stopped to check on Coco.

"Okay, we need time to remove the bandages, so there'll be no visitors until after six," she said before leaving.

"Thank you nurse," Coco said.

"Oh that's great," Deedee said, immediately forgetting about the news of Kim and Tina.

"It's about time," Josephine said. "I might just bring you a blunt."

"Nah, I'll be real high when they take these off, yo. I've bee waiting a long time to hear those words. You can't believe how happy I'll be. I ain't gonna need no weed."

"You sure? Shoot. I'm asking as if I know where to get it. Last week Showbiz and Silky Black had the studio reeking of some good shit. I caught a buzz soon as I walked in. Eric smelled that shit too," Josephine said with a chuckle.

"Silky Black and Showbiz are fine. Just tell him to get rid of the two hoochies. They're no good, yo."

"Coco, you sure you ain't hating? I spoke to Kim and Tina, they say—"

"Jo, I don't give a fuck wha them bitches say. They're no fucking good."

"You're right, Coco. I'll get my uncle to fire them immediately."

Josephine and Deedee walked to the elevator without a word spoken between them. While waiting silently for the elevator, Deedee suddenly walked back to the nurse's station. The elevator came and Josephine got inside with a mocking glare at Deedee.

CHAPTER 21

It was after five in the evening when Josephine arrived at the hotel. She tried to call Eric with no luck reaching him. Josephine was curious as to why he was in the Hamptons when he should be at work. It didn't make sense to her.

She soon met her mother in the lobby of the W Hotel. They planned on having an early dinner together. Josephine wanted to give her mother the reason why she couldn't leave New York.

Sitting silently at dining table, Josephine waited until they were finished eating before saying anything.

"You said you had something important to tell me. Well, what is it? We've got to leave tomorrow," her mother said.

"I'm not going back with you, mother. I have to stay here," Josephine said solemnly. She could feel her mother's cold stare ripping her apart.

"Why, Josephine?"

"Well because... because, I'm pregnant mother," she said, rushing the words.

Josephine momentary looked at her mother and their eyes met briefly. She saw the woman's head drop in agony.

"You'll have to have an abortion. I simply can't allow that. What about college? Your father and I both agreed for you to go Clark—"

"My father and you decided when? This is part of your court order, mother? I gotta live my life."

"You're pregnant and only seventeen and—"

"I'm eighteen, mother. Eighteen and legal," Josephine confirmed with attitude.

"Yes, you grew up fast, I guess."

"I was busy growing up while you were busy divorcing my father."

"You're still only a teenager."

"And what exactly does that mean?

"That means I'm still your mother, and I'm in charge of you."

"Didn't you tell me you started doing drugs and dating dad when you were a teen? Look at how your life turned out."

"Meaning what? Your father and I—"

"It means nothing is guaranteed in life except death, mother," Josephine deadpanned.

"You don't care about anyone but you."

"Who do you care about, mother?" Josephine asked and grabbed her handbag.

"Why—"

"You're not gonna stop me. I really don't wanna make a scene..."

"Who's the person that got you pregnant? Can I meet him?"

"He doesn't know anything yet, mother," Josephine said, looking away and staring off in space. "He'll find out soon," she continued with determination.

"I'll have to let your father know about this."

"That's fine. You can tell dad anything you want to."

"So this is what it's come down to? After all we've done for you? You turned into some damn unfavorable statistic. Is this the way you reward our sacrifices, Josephine? You're destroying your life, throwing away your future on some street hustler, I bet. All you want is to be somebody's baby mother? What about college? Career? Marriage?"

Josephine got up and walked away from the table. Her mother ran after her and quickly caught up.

"Don't you walk away from me when I'm talking to you. I'm still your mother, Josephine. You better show me some respect," she said too loudly. The heads of other diners turned to stare at the two.

"Oh, respect huh? You talk it but you've got to earn it mother. You're ready to plumb the depths of my soul, put me on a guilt trip. But I'm not taking it, mother. I'm old enough to do what I wanna. And this is where I get off," Josephine said and strutted away.

"Lemme get the bill, please," her mother impatiently said to the waiter, who was trying to keep them quiet.

"Just sign here. It'll be added to your tab," he said, shooing her out as soon as she signed the guest tab.

"Josephine! Josephine!" she cried, running from the dining area.

Josephine couldn't hear her mother. She really didn't care. Josephine was already in a cab headed back to the hospital to see Coco. Shortly before seven, she arrived and hurried to the elevator. Josephine's heels clicked loudly as she strutted down the hospital's hallway. She went inside the private room and closed the door. Deedee was sitting next to Coco's bed. They were laughing when Josephine entered. Then there was a pause filled with anxiety. Josephine stood at the door and stared at Deedee and Coco. It was Coco who said something first..

"Are you just gonna stand there or are you gonna come over here and give me a hug? I can see you, yo."

Josephine ran with arms outstretched to the bed. Coco got up and they embraced as Deedee watched with tears in her eyes. She joined them and they all started laughing, pointing at each other. It was a joyous moment. Coco had regained her sight and would leave the hospital soon.

"This calls for a lil' sump'n, sump'n," Josephine suggested.

"Whatcha got in mind, yo?" Coco asked.

"Well, this moment calls for a bud," Josephine said, pulling out a rolled blunt.

"Uh uh. You can't, crazy ass dame. This still a hospital, yo!"

"So who cares? It ain't like we burning down the place. We just gonna spark a lil' sump'n, sump'n."

"You got a point there, yo."

"I 'm not down," Deedee said.

"All we gotta do is light a cigarette just in case," Josephine cautioned.

"Hmm, good planning, yo."

"Y'all are both crazy," Deedee said, watching Josephine lighting the blunt and cigarette.

She puffed, puffed and passed the blunt to Coco. Deedee watched Coco taking the blunt and putting it between her lips. She inhaled so hard that for a moment her eyes rolled back into her head and she appeared stunned.

"Coco, are you okay?" Deedee asked as Coco tried to pass her the steaming blunt. "I don't want that shit," Deedee hissed.

Coco took another puff and whirled to hand it to Josephine. She seemed unbalanced.

"That shit got some kick to it. Where'd you cop that, yo?" Coco asked stumbling and falling as she turned.

"Are you alright Coco?" Deedee asked, rushing to help her up.

"I'm good. Just haven't smoked in a minute, that's all, yo."

Coco sat woozily on the bed as if dazed by the effect of smoking the blunt. She rocked back and forth.

"Coco, you want anymore?" Josephine asked. Coco wagged her finger waving her off. "I better clip this," Josephine said, putting out the blunt. It was then the door opened and the nurse walked in.

"What're you girls doing in here?" she thundered.

"Smoking? I'm gonna have to suspend your visiting privileges. There's absolutely no smoking anywhere in this hospital. Have you lost your minds?" she asked, picking up the smoldering cigarette and smelling it. She hurried to the bathroom and flushed it down the tiolet. "I think your visiting hours are over," she said to Deedee and Josephine.

Meanwhile, Coco sat on the bed with her vision completely blurred by the effects of marijuana. She started seeing black dots. Soon the dots became connected and the whole place went dark.

Josephine hurried out the hospital and jumped into a cab headed cross-town. She wanted to see Eric. Now she could face him. The cab pulled to a stop and Josephine paid and jumped out.

"Keep the change," she shouted, jumping from the cab and running inside the posh apartment building.

Josephine hurried to the floor and rang the doorbell, then waited with the side of her head pressed against the door. Her heart lifted when she heard the faint sounds coming from inside the apartment. Then she felt it sink deep into the pit of her stomach when she heard voices. The door opened.

"Hey, what're you doing here?"

It was Tina. Josephine was dumbfounded and opened her mouth but couldn't think of anything intelligent to say. Tina was clad in only bra and thong.

"Why you opening the door?" she heard Kim asking. Josephine saw she was also undressed down to her skivvies. Josephine was in total shock when she saw the man in the background. He said nothing, but what was there to say? She shook her head and took off running and screaming through the apartment, smashing television screens. Josephine went into the bathroom and scrawled on the bathroom mirrors. Then she left as Kim and Tina watched in horror.

"Bastard! You fucking bastard!" Josephine shouted running downstairs and out to the street. Stopping short of being hit by a bus, the emotional teen slowed her roll, walking while sobbing.

"He's doing both of them," she whispered to no one. "Are you okay?"

Josephine turned her head to see the silver Monte Carlo, windows down, decelerating to a crawl next her. She had seen his face before but couldn't care less.

"Is everything alright?" the man asked again.

"Yes, I'm fine. I'm fine, thank you," Josephine answered hurriedly. Picking up her pace, she tried hiding the tears stinging her face.

"Can I give you a ride somewhere?"

"No, I'll be alright," Josephine said and continued to walk.

"It's all good. I'm a detective." He smiled.

Josephine slowed her pace and stopped. She glanced inside the car and saw the detective's smiling face.

"Here's a Kleenex for those tears," he offered.

Josephine thought about it for a moment and then accepted

the offer. She got inside the car and the detective drove off.

“My name is Detective Kowalski,” he said with a wry smile.

“Oh, I know you,” Josephine started. “I remember you from that night outside the club…”

“You were coming from Eric Ascot, huh…?”

“That sex-starved bastard!”

“Oh?”

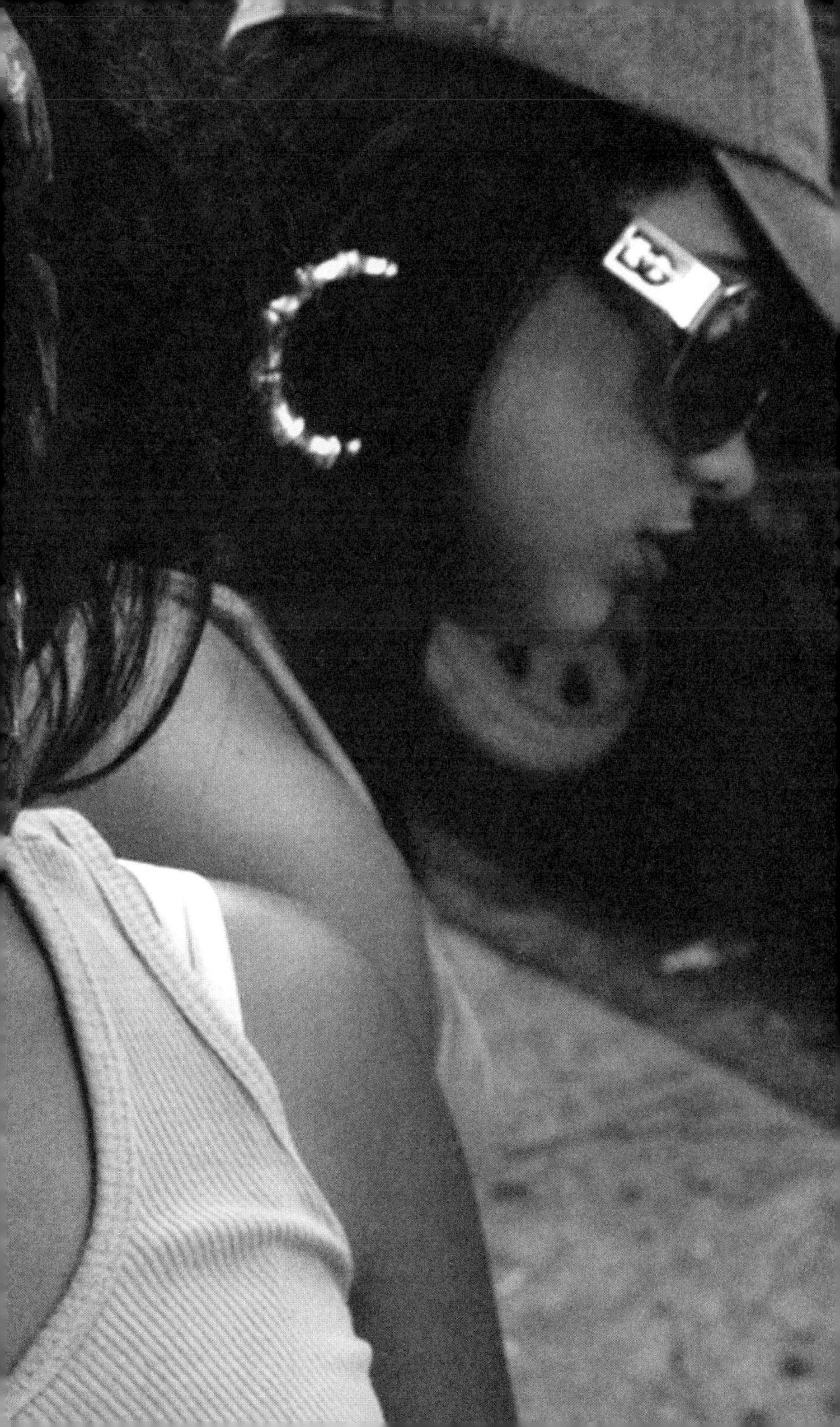

CHAPTER 22

The next morning, Eric sat inside his Hampton mansion thinking about his next move. He never got a response from the text message he had sent to Sophia and was about to call her when he saw Deedee's cellphone number flash up on his screen. Eric answered.

"Hi sweetheart," he said, then listened for a minute. "Fire them because of Coco's junior high school beef? Oh they tried to shoot you, huh? Are you sure? Alright we'll see. I'll see them later and find out. Okay sweetheart. Okay I'll be careful." Eric hung up and called his double in the studio from his home phone. "Hey I need you to do me a big favor today. I want you to monitor our receptionists. You were at my place with them last night? I told you not to take them there. Which car are you driving? Park the Rolls and pick up the Maybach. It's in a parking lot on Fifty-seventh and

Park," he said. "And one more thing, remember what—"

His cellphone was buzzing. Eric thought it was Sophia. "Hi," he said, picking up the incoming call without looking at the number. Josephine was on the other end ranting and raving. Eric listened for a sec. Then he put her on speakerphone. He returned to the conversation with his double. Josephine's voice could be heard revealing her most intimate desires.

"I love you Eric and showed you nothing but love. But I see now it was just sex to you. I'm just another notch under your belt. If you didn't want me, why did you do it? You're the older one here. You should think for both of us. I'm pregnant and that's it. I came to tell you that last night but you had other plans. And you don't have to lie because I saw you and those two ho's. All they do is tell lies and cover for you the way I used to. 'Mr. Ascot is not here,'" Josephine chided. Eric chuckled at the effectiveness of his deception. "Eric you lied to me. They told me you're at the studio and your niece said you were in the Hamptons."

"Why are you trying to find me, Josephine?"

"I love you and everything is going wrong in my life and I don't wanna lose you but last night when I saw you with them I ran outside and that detective ah…Kowalski, he just happened to be driving by and well he gave me a ride and we talked and he asked me questions about you and what I know about your connection with Lil' Long—"

"What you told the cops?" Eric asked, grabbing the phone and clutching it to his face. It was as if he had his hands around Josephine's neck. If he squeezed any tighter, the phone would've snapped like a twig. "What da fuck you told the police about me?

You stupid little bitch!"

"But Eric I didn't know anything was gonna happen. He just asked about Lil' Long. I wasn't here for that shit. That's hearsay, that's nothing in the court of law. Eric, I think I'm pregnant. We could have a little you. That makes you feel all warm inside, right Daddy? You can worry about paying your baby-mother's doctor's bills instead of your ex."

"Listen you stupid little girl. If you're pregnant, I'll pay for the abortion, but I don't want you around me anymore. I want you to stay away from me and my family. I don't want you calling my office, home or cellphone and I'm gonna get a court order against you."

"What? After all I've done. I don't want an abortion. Furthermore, I told 'em nothing. The police knew everything. C'mon Eric. You're acting like it was my fault. It was between you and Busta and Coco and Deedee and Lil' Long and his peeps. I wasn't there. What do I know?"

"I don't care. I'm gonna take out an order of protection against you."

"Yeah, run to the court, like a big bitch," Josephine said, going ballistica. "Who do you think they're gonna believe, you or me? You're a suspect in three murders. I'm a teenager who just graduated high school and you're having a sexual relationship with me, Mr. Big Shot. Who do you think they're gonna believe, huh?"

"You're crazy. You fucking need help. Get it soon."

"You're the one who's gonna need fucking help. Yeah, you done fucked up and they might be on their way any minute now to arrest your ass. And I hope you rot in jail, muthafucka... Eric,

Eric I didn't mean that. It's just that seeing you with them two ho's last night was just too much…"

"I told you it wasn't me—" Eric quietly chuckled at how she fell for his deception.

"Eric please, don't lie to me anymore. We've both made mistakes and we gotta work it out. Be there for me and I'll never again talk to the police about anything else," Josephine pleaded.

"Nah can do. I ain't fucking with you, bird-head. You're a serious risk. Fuck that! For all I know, you might start wearing a wire. Not that I got nothing to hide. I just want you to stay away from me, that's all."

The cellphone went dead in Josephine's hand. She clutched it closer to her ear.

"Hello, hello," she repeated.

Josephine redialed to no avail. Each attempted ring went to Eric's voicemail. After her sixth try, ended in frustration, Josephine vomited abuses at Eric through his voicemail.

"You fucking bastard. You will pay!"she screamed. Minutes later she called back screaming into her cellphone. "You're such a fucking liar. You were with them ho's, but Eric, I love you. I don't care about any bitches. Honey, I think it's all these fractured relationships I've been dealing with. Darling, I can forgive you and we can move on. Let's work this out, Eric. Please don't leave me alone. Don't do this to me. Call me."

Josephine threw the cellphone on the sofa just as her mother walked out of the bedroom. She packed a few things while Josephine seemed lost in her thoughts.

"Honey, you better start packing or we're gonna miss our

flight," she said in a hurried tone.

Josephine remained quiet and suddenly raced off to the bathroom. The door slammed shut. She quickly showered, slipped on black jeans and a clingy beige top. Josephine sat at the mirror slowly applying make-up. She ignored the knocking on the bathroom door. Thirty minutes later, Josephine faced her mother's inquiring stare.

"I'm not going with you, mother. I gotta stay in the city and settle some unfinished business," Josephine uttered almost inaudibly.

"Josephine, I want you to leave with me. I'll make everything like it used to be," her mother pleaded.

"I can't go mother. I'll join you soon," Josephine said, heaving her weekend Coach Bag onto her shoulder.

"Josephine, please wait…" her mother pleaded.

The teenage girl was already out the door, running to the elevator. She sighed and entered. Exiting the hotel, she found a cab and headed to the recording studio.

Josephine waited for a few minutes downstairs, trying to regain her composure before going upstairs to the recording studio. She fussed with her hair and got on the elevator. Josephine hopped off with her heart beat rapidly increasing. She saw Tina and Kim as soon as she walked in. They stared at her in bewilderment and both sighed when she spoke.

"Hi, I'm sorry about flipping like that last night but…"

"Look I don't care about shit but if it's Eric you came to see, he's not here," Kim said, greeting her with a suspicious stare.

"Okay, but can I go check for myself?"

"No way. You're not supposed to be up in here and those were strict orders. But we can't help because you were bitten by a teenage love bug and now you—"

"We don't do this normally but we'll let you slide because you were cool with us on our first day," Tina said with a wink. "Go take a look for yourself, girlfriend."

Josephine walked around the studio, checking the listening room twice and speaking to Reggie. She went into Eric's office and sat at his desk. Tina walked in.

"Okay, you gotta go now hon," she said, showing Josephine the door.

"I guess you're right. He's not here," Josephine said getting up and walking out. "I see you've been doing overtime," she sneered at Tina.

"So what? We just doing all the boss wants, baby doll," Tina said with a smile.

"Give it up, lil' sis, you're too young for him. Men like Eric with all that money are nothing but players. This game for grown ups. You keep hanging around and you're gonna get hurt, kid," Kim said.

"That's why you're fucking him? I'm pregnant for him, okay?" Josephine said, walking away.

Kim glanced at Tina for a second. They nodded to each other. Kim wrestled with the temptation of bodily throwing Josephine out.

"Please leave," Kim requested. Josephine smirked as she walked out the front door and headed to the elevator.

"Why you want us to be so nice to that bitch?" Kim angrily

asked Tina.

"Because that bitch could tell Eric that she saw us in his apartment fucking around with homeboy and homeboy may just say we brought that bag the DA gave us to leave at Eric's house. D'uh!" Tina snarled.

"Whatever, bitch. I wanna forget ever doing that shit again to anyone," Kim said.

"What? You getting cold feet, Kim. It's piece of cake. This shit will soon be over and Mike is already looking for a buyer for the diamond," Tina smiled.

"Who the hell is Mike?"

"Kowalski…"

"You told him bout it?"

"Hell to the muthafuckin' no you fool. Why would I? You and I are the only ones who knows I got that shit."

"You should've still let me put my foot up in that bitch's ass. Who she think she talking to?"

"Forget about that bitch. She's got that puppy love shit," Tina said.

Josephine was trembling with pent up anger and decided to wait downstairs for Eric. Fueled by her emotions, she sat in a nearby Starbucks sipping a latte, waiting. She glanced at the time. It was a little after two. The early afternoon sun was in full bloom along with flowers and birds chirping. Spring filled the air..

Lovers strolled, holding hands and stopping to kiss everywhere.

Couples were walking hand in hand, chatting on the busy sidewalk, all reminding her that she was alone. Josephine sat thinking about how to make up with Eric. She would make him laugh. He used to think she was funny. Her cellphone rang. Josephine checked and saw her mother's digits.

She was about to answer but ignored the call when she saw the black Maybach pulling into a parking spot. Lucky devil, she thought, smiling and putting away her cellphone. Only Eric could find parking on this busy street, Josephine thought as she got up and waved. He looked pass her as if she was invisible. She ran after him waving.

"Eric, Eric," she shouted, hurrying to catch up to the fast moving man.

"There goes da muthafucka right there," one man said, watching the scenario Josephine was causing. "Let's get this muthafucka, now."

"What about da bitch?"

"Fuck da bitch. She gets in da way, she gets hit up too. Let's creep on they asses."

Josephine was spitting curses to the man's back without paying any attention to what else was going on in the busy lunchtime sidewalk. She didn't see two men steadily creeping behind.

"Why you going by me like you don't know me? Dag! Can you at least help me with my bag? A few days ago you were getting blowjobs and fucking me, now you acting all new? Get da fuck outta here, Eric. I ain't one them ho's you fucking up in the studio. You a sex fiend. It s ménages in your apartment? That's what it is Eric? I'm just a jump-off, another notch under your belt…?"

"Huh? You must be crazy. I don't know... wha da fuck?" he responded without turning around or slowing down.

"Oh shit. Now you're gonna play me like that? I was just fucking you…" Josephine's voice trailed when the man turned around. That was when she realized it wasn't Eric.

"Who da fuck are you?" he quizzed.

"Oh shit! You driving his whips and wearing the same clothes but you ain't even Eric," she said with a baffled look. "Who da hell is you?"

Josephine's tirade and ignorance was curtailed by a barrage of bullets chopping her in half. She fell in a heap and Eric's panicked double ran but didn't get very far. Another outburst flung him forward and blew his upper torso to pieces. Flesh was all over the busy pavement. Pandemonium broke loose like a firecracker and pedestrians darted all over the place.

"I got him!" one of the hit men shouted as they made their getaway, running back to a parked car, jumping in and racing off.

Kowalski watched and pulled his gun, racing toward the scene. He got on his knees and fired two shots, hitting the driver, who crashed into an active crane. The blades of the forklift severed the passenger's head from his body. Kowalski pulled out his radio and spoke.

"We just lost a potential witness against Ascot, over" he said, looking at the mangled body of Josephine lying, leaking on the sidewalk.

CHAPTER 23

Coco sat up in bed and squinted, trying to see who was standing around her. Her vision was all fuzzy at first but she could hear the doctor's warnings.

"Don't try to strain your eyes to see, Coco. The muscles will get going. Let it come naturally. You feel funny and woozy but that's alright. It's the side effect from the eye drops. Don't try to run just yet and stay away from smoky places," the doctor smiled.

"You hear what the doctor's saying, cause I know how you like to smoke," Ms. Harvey said.

"Mother, you wanna chill for a minute?" Coco said, smiling at the faces staring at her. Deedee was there like always along with her annoying mother. Sophia came in to see her today and Eric was with her. Maybe that was the reason for Josephine's absence. It felt really good to survive the ordeal, Coco's thoughts were going. She heard the doctor's voice.

"Take these tablets and you'll be real fine. I think you can leave us today, Coco," the doctor continued.

"I'll make sure she takes them medications doc. You don't have to worry about that," Ms. Harvey said.

Deedee and Sophia smiled while Eric looked on proudly. It was the first time he had been there, but the flowers he sent filled her room. It was a real good feeling and Coco wore a big smile as Deedee hugged her and presented her with a topaz and white gold friendship ring. Coco slipped it on her finger.

"You're like my sis and I just want you to have that, Coco."

"Thank you, fam," she said holding, Deedee closely. "Oh, this is such a great day, yo."

"Yes, finally you can come home and let me cook for you so you could get some meat on your body. Coco, all she wants to eat is chocolate and munchies," Ms. Harvey said and the room laughed.

"Ma, why you putting me on front street like that, yo?"

"Don't start with that yo-ing street shit. Just because we in company I'll still have to get my respect," Ms. Harvey reminded her daughter.

"Okay, mother. I ain't trying to argue. All I wanna do is get outta here and get me a slice of pizza or sump'n."

"How about we get the whole pie?" Sophia suggested.

"I'm down," Deedee chimed in.

Ain't no one dumping on Jove…

You ain't in sanitation or sanitarium...

What're you crazy? Jay-Z will bury 'em...

The track rang out from the *S dot Collection*. Jay-Z's smooth rhymes came through the speaker and jolted everyone, except Coco.

"Turn that down. All this loud music while you're in the hospital. Can you imagine the noise she makes when she's home?"

"Yes, I can imagine," Eric smiled. "Speaking of which, stick this track in your headphone." Eric handed a CD to Coco. "Let the beat marinate in your head. I was thinking about you when I heard it."

Coco already had the disc banging in her headphones. She nodded her head to it and smiled.

"Nice beat. Tougher than dice... my name's Coco and I'm tougher than dice..." she rapped nodding her head.

"You best take it easy before you pass out," Ms. Harvey cautioned.

"Your mother is right. Maybe you should save it for later," Sophia said.

"Uncle E. and Coco are always listening to music. There has to be some kind of sound going," Deedee laughed, hugging her uncle and Coco.

"Well... seeing how y'all helped Coco and myself go through this. I mean because I've being going through a lot with this and that on my mind. And I'm truly happy that y'all stepped up the way y'all did. I mean everyone. Sophia, Deedee and Eric. Y'all stepped up real big for us. And I just wanna say thanks to y'all."

Eric's cellphone started ringing loudly.

"Thank God for cellies, yo," Coco smiled and winked. "I really like this beat."

"Anyone can tell you love your uncle but you have a lot of respect for him too," Ms. Harvey said to Deedee.

"Yes, she's her uncle's girl," Sophia deadpanned.

"You should marry this beautiful, nice lady here," Ms. Harvey said to Eric, who was still on the cellphone.

"This is where I've got to leave," the doctor said. "I'll make my rounds and Coco, I'll be back to sign your release as soon as you're ready and packed."

"Thank you Dr. Gluckmann," Coco said. She got out of the bed and made a few shaky steps toward the doctor. She hugged him. "Thanks," she said.

"Thank you very much, doctor," Ms. Harvey said. "And most of all thank you God for saving my daughter. Because without you she wouldn't be with us…" Ms. Harvey's voice trailed as she became too emotional to continue.

"Ms. Harvey, you better get her home and get her a lot of rest. Coco, I got some phat new beats for you to groove on," Eric said, closing his cellphone and walking out the room with the doctor. Sophia moved in and praised Ms. Harvey's motherly love.

"You're a good mother and you really do care about your daughter," she said, hugging Ms. Harvey. "I'm happy for you and Coco."

"Ma, you looking sharp," Coco observed. "What's that

Coach gear? And where is that coming from?"

"I've been shopping in Deedee's closet," Ms. Harvey laughed.

"For real?"

"She's been hanging," Deedee smiled.

"Oh don't get her started, yo," Coco cautioned. "She's a beast."

They all laughed and helped Coco pack. The group walked out and headed to the parking lot. Sophia drove with Deedee inside a black Bentley Continental. Coco and her mother traveled in the Rolls Royce Phantom driven by Eric. Her mother was busy admiring the car while Coco was getting used to seeing all the people. She could smell the sidewalk trade of the city, the freshly roasting nuts and bagels. She closed the window as the cars made a pit-stop at Ray's pizzeria and they ordered several pies.

The mood was festive when they pulled up in the parking lot of Eric's posh apartment building. Deedee jumped out the car and assisted Coco to the elevator. The group went upstairs and inside.

Eric opened the door and dropped the boxes of pizzas on the floor. He stared around the apartment in pained astonishment. The place was a wreck. Television screens were all broken and glass was shattered everywhere. All were shocked and walked around the place speechless.

"What the fuck happened!" Eric exclaimed after a while.

"I don't know," Deedee answered, looking around.

"Looks like a robbery, yo," Coco quipped.

"I don't think so. There's a message on the bathroom mirror from Josephine," Sophia said.

"Josephine?" Eric echoed. The doorbell rang.

"I'll get it," Deedee smiled. She opened the door and three detectives strode in. They went directly to Eric and stood looking at him.

"We have a warrant for your arrest, Mr. Ascot. You have the right to remain silent..."

"This is harassment,' Eric yelled.

"Why are you so nervous, Mr. Ascot?" one of the detectives asked.

"I should be. There are four white guys with badges and guns uninvited at my apartment. Any black man would be intimidated."

The detective placed handcuffs on the shocked Ascot and Kowalski went directly to a Gucci duffel bag. He casually pulled out a couple kilos of cocaine as Eric's eyes widened in disbelief. Astonishment registered on Sophia's face. Ms. Harvey was in shock. Coco and Deedee watched frozen in place.

"That ain't even my bag! What da fuck is this?"

"If this is your apartment, you're responsible for everything in here. We got a tip you're holding weight but we didn't expect this much," Kowalski smiled.

"Enjoy your meals, ladies," one of the detectives said as they pushed Eric out the door.

"They can't do that!" Deedee screamed in aguish. "It's not fair," she sobbed.

Coco walked to where she stood and touched her

shoulder. They remained silent for several beats. Deedee turned and hugged Coco. They held each others' embrace for a few minutes before letting go. Sophia and Ms. Harvey were holding hands when the girls approached them.

"He didn't look like any drug dealer. You can tell he wasn't into breaking any laws," Ms. Harvey said, hugging the distraught and disappointed Sophia.

"What do we do now?" Deedee asked.

"C'mon, I'll take you and your mom home, Coco. You'll need your rest."

Later when Sophia pulled to a stop, Deedee hugged Coco and Ms. Harvey.

"I never thought I'd be happy to see this building," Coco said, holding on to her mother.

"He's gonna be alright. Them cops are assholes, they just trying to frame him," Ms Harvey said taking Coco's bag.

Coco and her mother waved and they walked toward the building. Several onlookers greeted the pair.

"I'm so happy to see the sign that say out of order," Coco chuckled as she saw the familiar signs of her apartment building and fell on the sofa. She sat thinking about how lucky she'd been. Her mother sat next to her.

"Welcome home," Ms. Harvey, said turning on the television. "Those people may be very rich but they have a lot of problems," she noted.

"Mo money, mo problems. Biggie said that," Coco said.

"I don't care what Biggie say. Lemme watch some TV and get my mind off all that mess."

Tina was in Kim's living room waiting confidently. She smiled and poured beer in a glass. Kim walked in as she put the glass to her lips.

"Why don't you just drink the beer from the bottle? You be dirtyin' ma shit and never clean nothing," Kim said.

"Chill girlfriend. Soon you'll be hiring a dozen maids and shit. Then what you're gonna say?"

"I'm gonna say get out of my place. And when is that crazy ass cop coming? He called you yet?"

"This might be him right now," Tina said. "Let's go downstairs and talk big money. We're gonna be rich."

"Where's the ice?"

"I got that baby right here," Tina said, pointing to her Luis Vuitton purse.

They exited and waited a few minutes for Kowalski to pull around. Tina got in the front and Kim sat in the backseat. Kowalski drove off smiling. He seemed to be in an unusually good mood. Kim eyed him suspiciously.

"You girls did really good work," Kowalski smiled at Tina. "It went down perfect. Our suspect is cozy behind bars and now I'm gonna buy y'all dinner."

"What about the money for the diamond?" Tina asked smiling.

"That's another matter. Let's discuss it after dinner,"

Kowalski said.

The three ate at a small diner at Frank's Steakhouse and Chicken, a quiet eatery with big parking lot, next to Harlem's Polo Ground. Throughout the entire fried chicken meal, Kim kept watching Tina's nervousness. She tried touching her leg but Tina refused to acknowledge her.

"I'm going to the bathroom," Kim stood and announced while staring at Tina. It was clear she wanted Tina to join her. "Don't you need to go to the bathroom too?" Kim asked Tina. Finally, they picked up their pocketbooks and walked away together.

"You gave him that fucking diamond didn't you? Just tell me the truth, Tina," Kim pleaded when they were inside the ladies room. Tina didn't answer and tried to avoid Kim's cold stare. She fixed her make-up. "We went and set up someone and he don't even wanna talk about the diamond and I knew it, I knew it… you gave that cop the rock, didn't you?"

"We're gonna get paid," Tina said confidently. "Let's finish and later we'll find out how much."

They went back and finished having their meals. Kowalski paid the tab and by the time they left a cloud of tension hung over the three.

"Mike, tell us how much we getting," Tina said anxiously.

"I was told twenty thousand dollars," he said. "Ten for me and here's your ten right here."

He handed Tina an envelope with the money and Kim whistled a loud sigh. Kowalski started the car and glanced at her.

"Twenty thousand is twenty thousand," he stated.

Kim looked at him from the corner of her eyes. She didn't want to tell him how she felt but her rage spilled out.

"How's it gonna be only twenty thousand? The reward alone for it is like two hundred thou," Kim snarled. "You trying to play us!"

The whack across her cheek shut her up immediately and caused her lips to bleed. Kim gave him the coldest stare she could muster.

"Don't you ever talk like that to me again, you bitch!"

"Mike, chill., She didn't mean…"

"You know better than talking to me, slut!"

"Mike all she meant was that... twenty thousand, that's all you got for the diamond?"

"That goes for you too," he said angrily.

Kowalski kept the engine idling and stared at Tina. She realized he was lying to her about the reward money and nothing he said would changed it. Kowalski tried.

"I had to make a deal with some of my friends to keep your asses from being set up for robbery," he lied. "I couldn't just walk in and tell them you took the diamond. Fucking, twenty thousand is a lot of dough in any language."

"It ain't enough, Mike. It just ain't," Tina said, shaking her head.

"I can't believe we did all that work for these cops and on top of that you gave him the diamond," Kim said.

"How else would she get the money? Are you stupid? They're not gonna give the reward money unless the merchandise is handed back."

"You gave him the diamond, huh Tina?"

"Yes, I did. I had to," Tina said to Kim. Then she looked at Kowalski. "I thought we had a deal?"

"You know better than to trust the police," Kim sneered.

"What're you gonna do now?" Kowalski asked.

Kim heard the sudden blast and saw Kowalski clutching his face. She saw Tina clutching a .45 caliber and cocking the slide. Another round chambered. The gun glinted from the streetlight. Kim heard the deafening gunshots rang out twice. She stared in wide-eyed surprise at Tina without saying anything. The shooter rifled the pockets of the dead detective. Kim jumped out of the still idling car wiping brain matter and flesh off her clothing.

"You shot the fucking cop!" Kim screamed. "My fucking ears still ringing, bitch!" she yelled. "You could've let me know."

"Chill. That nigga deserved it," Tina said contemptuously.

"What're you gonna do with the gun?"

"I'm a leave it at the Eric's studio. They gonna think he did it anyway."

"Let's get da fuck up outta here before somebody spots us."

They walked away leaving the detective with his face in a mass of blood, sitting in the idling car.

"You're a fucking idiot," Kim said as they hurried out of the area.

It was late evening and Coco's mother had fallen asleep next to her. The television blared and Coco quickly located the remote. She was about to lower the volume when the late news caught Coco's well rested eyes. She saw the faces and knew immediately something bad had happened to Josephine.

"Coco, turn that down," her mother shrieked.

Coco heard the news confirming her worse fears. It was being broadcast the day of her release from the hospital.

"Investigations are still on the way in the shooting of two people in midtown earlier today. Eyewitnesses described the two people killed in a hail of gun fire…Josephine Murray, an aspiring singer and model Derek Miles were struck down by a fusillade of automatic weapons, in what police are calling a botched hit…the police are still investigating at this time…"

Coco listened for a few minutes and then realized Ms. Harvey was awakened by the telephone ringing off the hook.

"Is that your other friend?" Ms. Harvey asked, walking to get the phone. "We were just eating dinner with her the other day. I wonder what happened. She looked like she got mixed up with the wrong set of people," Ms. Harvey said, then picked up the telephone.

"Hello," Ms. Harvey said. "It's Deedee," she said, giving the phone to Coco.

"There's so much drama. Did you see the news, yo?

That's what you called about, right yo? That's fucked up!" Coco said grabbing the telephone confused.

"Coco, please fuckin' remember where you are," Ms. Harvey reminded.

"I can't believe it. I can't believe that shit really happened. I was just watching the news and the fucking shit hit me like pow!" Coco said. She covered the phone. "I'm soo sorry, ma. Yo Dee, I'm a call you back, yo. I gotta finish watching this."

It was all over the evening news. Bits and pieces of the report of the shooting were on the local channels. But nothing altered the fact that Josephine had been shot down in the streets. She was dead and Coco's steady stream of tears flowing down her face couldn't bring her back. Coco quietly munched on a chocolate bar, watching the streets down below. She could see people moving back and forth in the shadows and felt the gnawing emptiness deep down inside her.

"Don't stay up all night, Coco," her mother shouted.

Coco returned to the table. She sat down with pen and pad in hand. Her tears wet the empty sheet. She slowly scrawled Josephine, Danielle and Coco on the paper. Da Crew she wrote below their names, and stuck the *Tougher Than Dice* CD in her headphone. The beat was pumping and Coco put pen to paper.

My sisters dream about us being on the top, our hopes will not die cuz through me you'll always fly/ Things sometimes don't always work out the way we plan but I'm taking a stand/ I'm gonna do what's right/ My sisters will live through me cuz I ain't going down without a fight/ I know things gonna go my way/ I'll have all I want on lock/ Up in da club hanging in the back/ Another sold out performance reminiscing bout da crew how we used to put it down/ My time's now this the moment I'm ready to run shit/ Handling things like a real hood chick/ Take me out the ghetto I'm still soo hood/ For my peeps who lost their lives/Never taking shit for granted coming in as the greatest I swear/ only thing that bothers me is my girls ain't here...

Coco stopped writing and wondered aloud in a hoarse whisper, "Why they had to die?" She bowed her head in deep thought and took the headphones off. With her eyes closed, she was staring into an abyss of infinite possibilities. Coco was searching for the solution to a gnawing she felt in her gut.

She broke down crying and started reminiscing over Danielle and Josephine. They were Da Crew and it was the final of the teen talent competition of last summer.

"Here we go; ladies and gentlemen. Our final finalists for you are Da Crew!"

The three girls ran to the center of the stage and were met by flashing, bright lights. Coco, Danielle and Josephine attacked the stage, marking their territory like cats, making it difficult for anyone else to follow their tracks.

Danielle sang and moaned her way into every heart, while Coco rapped soul to go. Her words flowed like no ordinary rapper. She was vicious in her lyrical assault, taking no prisoners but holding the audience hostage. Josephine provided smooth background vocals and hammered out a rap. Her steps and moves deceived and delighted the naked eye.

The audience were caught napping. They slept through six lullabies and the seventh rocked them. Club kids jumped to their feet, moving with the heavy rhythmic beat. They clapped their hands, even while they sought refuge from the heat of Da Crew. There was no shelter from the storm and they were even more hyped when Coco shouted into the microphone.

"An old lady told me to knock out da competition, leave 'em dead, blood oozing from their fucking heads, rolling off with lyrics. Kicking like Bruce. My vocabulary is like a fist of fury. What I come to say is me and Da Crew ain't fucking here to play. Tell you something, you hear?. All y'all want mo? Well, let me give ya my girl, Jo."

It went big with a pop for Da Crew. They renewed the onslaught of the Chop Shop Crew, whose members took notice and began discussing the girls' performance.

"Yo, honeys could open for us."

"No question. Ghey'll do a lil' sump'n, you know?"

"Yo, we should find out who managing them. They nice."

"Muthafuckin' right!"

"They got all the moves too."

Busta, Eric Ascot, Sophia and Deedee were upstairs in a booth watching the video feed. They witnessed Da Crew, re-run after re-run.

"They were without question the best," Eric noted.

"I told ya they butters," Busta bragged. "Them judges are gonna have to give those six other acts honorable mention or

sump'n. C'mon, lemme go see how they doing."

An elevator took them down to where the finalists nervously waited. Deedee walked to Da Crew and hugged the girls. Eric, Busta and Sophia shook each finalist's hand, wishing them all good luck.

Josephine noticed the gesture. "Everyone is so cool tonight," she said excitedly. "I'm so tired, but it feels great, like this should go on forever. This really cool."

The four girls continued hugging. Eric and Busta kissed each girl on the cheek.

"You were the best. Your show was damn great," Eric said.

"Yeah, you were the best," Busta said enthusiastically. "I can't dispute da truth," he laughed.

While Deedee and Sophia chatted with Da Crew, Eric and Busta wandered off to meet the other guests and judges.

"I'm saying, yeah, I'd love to work with Da Crew," Eric said confidently.

"Yeah, well then that's that. You know they won. You've seen the response. Let's check what the judges say," Busta said. There was a burst of music, then the booming sound of the emcee's voice.

"We've got Eric Ascot in da house tonight."

"And his niece, Deedee! Yea-a-ah!" Deedee shouted.

Da Crew laughed along. The girls began pacing around, forming their usual circle, accompanied by Deedee and Sophia.

"Wonder what's taking so long, yo?"

"Yeah, it's only seven acts to choose from," Danielle said.

"Hmm, I don't like all this waiting around. For what?" Josephine pondered.

Coco lit another cigarette and sat on the floor. She seemed tired. Deedee noticed and went off to get two sodas. She returned, sat next to Coco and gave her one. The pair watched Josephine and Danielle attracting all the young boys.

"If they give this to anyone else, oh, it'd be a major diss," Deedee said.

"It's close to that time," Danielle said.

"What time is that?" Josephine asked.

"Our time..!" they shouted, high-fived and laughed while jumping around.

"This is Da Crew's hour!" Coco, Danielle and Josephine shouted.

"And the top three finalists are..." the booming voice of the emcee announced, behind a thunderous drum-roll. Da Crew heard the names of other finalists. Suddenly everyone was kissing and hugging them. They won and the crowd converged on them, mobbing them.

Coco spotted Josephine and Danielle hugging in the flashing lights. They signaled to her and she disengaged from Deedee's embrace and ran to the center of the stage to join them. Camera lights flashed and applause thundered in the air. Coco, Danielle and Josephine repped Da Crew, smiling, holding hands and taking a final bow, relishing their shine in the spotlight.

To be continued

GHETTO GIRLS V: *TOUGHER THAN DICE*

Enjoy this Excerpt from BlacKout the Novel
In Stores Now!!

ONE

August 14, 2003, 8:00 a.m.

The people of Flatbush, Brooklyn awoke to the sweltering heat coming off the top of the apartment buildings. Sunshine and high humidity locked the city in a ferocious heat vice. Craving relief, the residents of Browser Street migrated from their apartments to enjoy the fresh air outdoors.

It was around 9 a.m. when three women of West Indian descent sat on lawn chairs blocking the entrance to 254 Browser Street. They were busy chatting up the latest gossip, while keeping their eyes on the crowd of teens surrounding Tech. He was in front of the barbershop hawking his CDs and DVDs.

"I got it all," Tech shouted. "From the latest Fifty to classic Biggie, some new Jay-Z, I got it ... I got it!"

By 10:00 a.m., Corey was on his way to the barbershop to get a haircut, and stepped to Tech with a request.

"What it do? You have the new *Bad Boys II* soundtrack?" Corey asked checking out Tech's display.

"I got it right here, dog!" Tech said handing the CD to Corey.

“That joint’s bananas,” Tech added as Corey examined the disk. “It’s selling like crack all day long, everyday,” Tech said pushing his sales pitch.

“Hmm…word? What it do?” Corey asked.

“On n’ poppin’! Cop it. It’s jumpin’. And you need this Sean Paul remix and the G-Unit and Fifty Cent joint… Fire!” Tech said placing two CDs in Corey’s hand.

“Ahight, I hear you,” Corey said looking at each CD and quickly passing a twenty dollar bill to Tech.

“And I got the new Freddy versus Jason on DVD, director’s cut! Fire! What you know about that?”

“Damn! That joint ain’t due out for another couple weeks,” Corey said scratching his head, visibly impressed.

“What’s my muthafucking name, dog?” Tech asked.

“Ahight, you do what ya do, dogs,” Corey said smiling and giving Tech a pound.

Nelson and Rick lifted the gate to the barbershop, triggering a sudden flight of pigeons from their overnight perches.

“Whew, its gonna be a mother of a hot one today. You feel the heat already?” Nelson observed, shielding his eyes and gazing at the bright sun.

“Yeah, no doubt. I’m sayin’ my brother, may we shine like the sun,” Rick nodded in agreement. “Hope we get a lot of heads today,” he added walking inside and dusting off his barber chair.

"What it do?" Corey greeted, walking into the barbershop. "I need a fresh one for the weekend, Rick," he continued, taking a seat in Rick's chair and glancing at the mirror.

The barbershop was the place where everyone who was anyone came to hang out. From the latest cuts to freshest style, anything that was popping happened first at Nelson's barbershop.

Nelson was a proud, thirty-something entrepreneur who owned the barbershop. A vocal leader, he had street savvy with genuine social conscience. He was known to stand up for friends and often went out of his way to give a helping hand. At the same time, Nelson had old-school swagger and was known to get down with his knuckle game. He made his reputation fighting for what he believed in.

Rick, one of Nelson's barbers, was also in his thirties and had the rep of being an entertaining brother. Known for his sometimes arrogant ways, Rick enjoyed yapping about his sexual exploits. His different baby mothers would sometimes show up at the barbershop bringing drama. Most of the customers just laughed at his calamities, while he busily laced another satisfied customer with the latest fresh haircut.

Cam was the only female hanging in the group. She was a star athlete in high school, renowned for her basketball prowess. Her talent on the court earned her mad respect from the fellas. She wasn't at the barbershop for haircuts; it was simply her favorite hangout. Not only did Cam enjoy hanging with them, she also dressed like one of the guys, sporting baggy jeans, T-shirt and corn rows.

"Damn, look at the ass on shortie in that video! She doin' what she do," Corey said pointing to the television screen.

For a few rump-shaking seconds, all eyes turned to look at the latest Jigga video playing on BET.

"You know I heard them chicks don't make a dime, shaking ass in those videos, you feeling me?" Nelson announced.

"I don't know about all that. I know they gotta to be eating. I used to date one of'em video-hos, I mean 'chicks', and I'm sayin', the bitch was getting paid," Rick said smiling.

"Yeah, video-ho is right. They getting paid for their services off camera, that's what's really up," Cam said sucking her teeth.

"Sounds a little like hatin', you feel me, Cam?" Nelson smirked.

"Please, I don't love 'em ho's. I likes me a gangsta bitch. I like'em pretty but gangsta, that's what's up," Cam smiled.

"Damn, I'm sayin', you might as well just date a dude," Rick said with a chuckle.

Cam's explanation was drowned by raucous laughter. She resigned herself to throwing up her two middle fingers.

Tech took a break from hustling and walked into the barbershop. He and Nelson were very good friends and shared much history. Both had played on the same high school basketball team and came up hustling drugs with each other. After getting caught up with the law, they both got out the game.

Besides selling mixed CDs, Tech also functioned as the manager for budding rapper L. Tech not only assisted with sales and marketing of his new CD, he was also helping to get L signed to a recording deal with a major label. Tech worked at a friend's makeshift recording studio on Flatbush Avenue and was able to print a couple thousand CDs and sell them. The partnership was going well, but L needed to manage his time better. This is where Tech's help was crucial.

"Where's your boy L? He ain't here yet?" Tech asked Nelson.

"How long have you known L?" Nelson shot back.

"A while now," Tech answered with a chuckle.

"You know that nigga in the bodega messing with them Arabs, or rollin' up sump'n to smoke, " Nelson said.

"That's one hun'red. L's probably at the bodega gettin' a Dutch or sump'n," Tech said.

"You feel me? He does nothing but roll up, gettin' high on bullshit all day long," Nelson laughed.

"He'll be here soon, high as a muthafucka, talking plenty shit. And that's one hun'red," Tech laughed.

The two men exchanged dap like friends who had shared many years of private jokes between them, and Tech went back to work.

"Come get these CDs," Tech shouted to passersby while looking out for L.

AUGUSTUS
PUBLISHING
WHERE
HIP-HOP
LITERATURE
BEGINS...

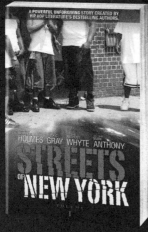

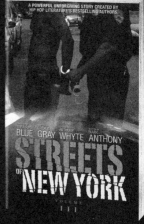

Written By
Anthony Whyte
Jerry LaMothe
BlacKout
CASWELL COMMUNICATIONS
BlacKout
THE NOVEL
ESSENCE BESTSELLING AUTHOR
ANTHONY WHYTE
BASED ON SCREENPLAY BY JERRY LaMOTHE